D1277253

A DOPEBOY'S TRASH, A PLUG'S TREASURE

L. RENEE

A Dopeboy's Trash, A Plug's Treasure

Copyright 2019 by L. Renee

Published by Mz. Lady P Presents, LLC

All rights reserved

This book is a work of fiction. Names, characters, places, and incidents either are the product of the author's imagination or are used fictitiously and are not to be construed as real. Any resemblance to actual persons, living or dead, business establishments, events, or locales or, is entirely coincidental.

No portion of this book may be used or reproduced in any manner whatsoever without writer permission except in the case of brief quotations embodied in critical articles and reviews.

ACKNOWLEDGMENTS

First, I will always thank God for my many blessings and opportunities I've been given. After years I am living my dream and building my career. I want to thank my family and friends for the continued support I truly appreciate it. Book 5 and many more to come from me.

My MLPP Pen sister's I love you ladies and we have all been grinding and working and I can't wait until the charts have of us all up there where we belong. It's so much talent and dopeness in one company. This is our time to keep growing we got this ladies love you girls.

Mz. Lady P A.K.A Boss Lady I admire you and I appreciate you so much. You teach us and guide and have never steered me wrong from book 1 to now with book 5 and I am honored to be a part of your company.

Ariel A. Gavin you are truly a gem and I am forever grateful for the many talks and help you have given me. We have built a bond from being Pen Sisters, but you are truly a friend for life and I know we gone keep grinding until we get to where we belong on them charts. Keep writing them Bomb ass books and tell your readers that my Hubby off limits Book bae or not lol I love you sis.

Vinee Raynell my dope poet pen sis thank you for being a sounding board and listener to me on many ideas and things I wanted to do. I started doing these book covers just playing around, but you have been right there cheering me on and I appreciate you. Love you boo.

My momanger the best mother a girl could ask for. I love and appreciate you. You been supportive and on board since day one and I love you to the moon and back.

Last but not least my readers. The amount of love and feedback I have got from books has been amazing. I never expected to have true readers checking for my next release and I hope you all enjoy this book. Love L. Renee The Author

I dedicate this book to every person who has ever experienced heartbreak. It may seem as if you are lost but never give up on yourself or love.

SYNOPSIS

One man's trash is another man's treasure is how the saying goes. In Treasure Belmont's case that literally rings true. Treasure dropped everything to move to Miami with her man Shyne who happens to be a Dopeboy. What once was a good idea to her soon becomes the one move, she regrets. A series of events will reveal Shyne's deceit and blatant disrespect for their relationship. While this feels like the ending. Unbeknownst to Treasure it's her new beginning in the form of a new man by the name of Honour.

Sparkle Reynolds has secrets that could be deadly if found out by her Ex Goose. At one point in life Goose was her everything. But everything that glitters ain't gold. Starting over and living for herself Sparkle ends up in Miami living across the hall from Treasure. The two build a bond and friendship.

Sparkle and Treasure are having the time of their lives dealing with new found love and getting back to their happy place. The happiness they've found so hard to get may be ruined with their bitter ex's plotting against them.

Will their happiness be torn apart by men scorned or will the men who have brought happiness into these women's lives handle the problem? Follow Treasure and Sparkle as they find out what it means to be loved beyond measure. They'll learn what it's like to be one man's trash and another man's treasure.

Chapter One

TREASURE

I stayed up twenty-four hours straight because my mind was racing, and my heart was hurting. I know I am partly to blame for my hurt, but Shyne promised me that last time was the last time he'd do me like this. I moved out here to Miami with him while he chased his dope boy dreams. I had no one close here to confide in except my neighbor Sparkle. She was cool, but she never wanted to go out or do anything. We were young and in Miami, the party city, but hardly went to the beach, let alone a party. My mother told me not to leave with this nigga, but at twenty, I thought I was grown and found the love of my life. Shyne treated me good for the first two years, and there wasn't a soul that could tell me he didn't love me.

Nevertheless, here we were five years into it, and I didn't know who he even was anymore. He wasn't coming home at night anymore, sometimes days in a row. I knew then that he had to be cheating because we don't know many people out here, and he wasn't sleeping in the trap. I knew that from the multiple times that I popped up there, and he was nowhere to be found. Tonight, I had no energy to go looking for him though. I honestly wanted out of this one-sided relationship, and now was the time to break free. While he was laid up with god knows who, I could make a dash for it and never look back.

I was tired of the lies the private phone calls and the vandalizing of my car more times than I can count, but who was I kidding, I wasn't going anywhere. Shit, I couldn't go anywhere. I ain't have nowhere to go yet, and I refused to move back home.

I didn't have anything of my own to get up and leave with, and for that reason, I was stuck where I was because I let a man provide and control me. Today I was deciding to set myself up in a position to leave and do for myself. There wasn't any love left in this house, and I was starting to think there never really was. Shyne hadn't touched me in weeks, let alone made love to me in years. It was a time he couldn't keep his hands off me, and I never felt lonely. The sad truth is Shyne always was a rude ass nigga though, but my silly, young, and dumb ass loved it back then.

I got out my laptop and started researching culinary schools. I always enjoyed cooking and baking, so what better time than now to go to school and start my dream career. I wanted a catering business restaurant, bar, and bakery. Today was the first day of the rest of my life. I decided to focus this time and energy that I wasted crying and hurting over Shyne in building my myself up and over.

I sent a text to Sparkle to see if she wanted to go with me to tour the few schools I found, and she said she was down, so I decided to get dressed and start my day off more positive despite this nigga making my life negative and draining. As of today, it's fuck Shyne. It's all about Treasure from here on out.

Chapter Two

SPARKLE

I decided to pull my hair back and wear my snapback hat and matching shades. I was starting to get used to the beautiful weather in Miami, and I couldn't wait to feel comfortable to enjoy it. I had been in Miami for six months now after I had to pack up for the third time and leave everything behind. I ran off almost two years ago from my abusive ex-husband, and when a friend of his ran into me, I had to pick up and leave before he found out it was me and my secret was revealed. Two years ago, I faked my death and started a new identity. If Goose knew I was still alive, he would surely kill my ass for real this time.

I met Goose when I was working as a lookout girl for a local drug dealer in our neighborhood. I was sixteen. My mother was sick. She had a terminal illness, and I had to provide for us. My father was in jail serving twenty years for killing the man who killed his mother. They called it a crime of passion and diagnosed my father with mental illness. He would be home in a few years, and I know he was looking for me once the money and letters stopped and my number changed.

When my mother died, Goose was my shoulder to cry on. He helped me get my first place, which became our first place, and soon we were a couple. He made me stop hustling, and I went to school and got my degree as a pharmacist, but he never let me work to use it.

I thought I had the perfect man until Goose became possessive and violent with me. As time went on, it only got worse, and as my young body developed, he began to really trip over anything I wore and anywhere I tried to go. It got to the point where all I did was sit in the house depressed and ready to end it all. One day I watched a Lifetime movie and got the idea to fake my death. I was able to convince Goose to let me work part-time because I was too bored. I used the time wisely and didn't really work part-time but per diem at the local CVS. I retrieved a dummy mannequin and started my plan.

One night I told him I was called in for a late shift, and my plan was set in motion. I drove my car close by work off the freeway where I had paid a crack head to crash into my car for $200. After he left the scene, I set the mannequin dressed like me and the one dressed like an older lady in the other car. I had spent good money ordering these life-like dolls on the black web. I dressed the doll in my pharmacy coat and badge, and I made sure my identical lace front was on there as well. I put the wedding rings and the jewelry and my purse and cell phone. I poured gas over the two crashed vehicles and tossed a match before I hightailed it with a book bag, new identity, and a new cell phone.

I had a bus ticket under my new name, Sparkle Reynolds, and I was never looking back. That was almost two years ago, and so far, no one here in Miami knew a thing. I only talked to my neighbor Treasure and my therapist because I suffered severely with depression and paranoia. I felt like any day he would come and find me. I broke away to live yet i was barely living at all. Something has got to give; it made no sense I was still confined to my home after getting away from goose.

Chapter Three

SPARKLE

I was up early doing my home workout in my spare room that I made a gym when there was a knock at my door. Out of habit, I retrieved my gun from my hiding spot in my closet and placed it in the small of my back. I crept to the door and checked through the peephole. I was instantly relieved when I saw my friend and neighbor Treasure on the other side of my door. I relaxed and opened the door up and Treasure, smiling brightly, pranced right in like a runway model. She was carrying a box of cannolis from the bakery in our building and a glass pitcher of her homemade mimosa punch that has become my favorite Sunday pick me up.

We never hung out anywhere other than each other's apartments, the gym in our building, and at the pool. That was all my doing. I didn't want to risk being seen by anyone that knew Goose. I hoped that one day this all would pass so that I could live my life not confined to my home. Surprisingly though, Treasure never pressured me for us to go out. I grabbed the box of cannolis from her and headed to the couch. I turned off the workout video and turned on *The Real* talk show. Treasure poured us some glasses of the mimosa punch and joined me in the living room on the couch. We talked and laughed about everything for almost an hour or so before she started to tell me the story about what Shyne had done this damn time.

"Sparkle, I am putting my plan in place, and as of today, I will be moving on. I must leave this nigga alone before he drives me insane. I can't keep doing these drives by his trap spots and pulling up at the club acting a whole fool and a half out here. Nah, I'm over that shit. I got me a nice little amount of money saved up, so I will be getting me a place tucked off where he doesn't know where it is. I'ma change my number and just ghost his ass. I promise that because I can't do this shit no more man."

She blew out air in frustration as she wiped the tears from her eyes. I passed her the box of Kleenex.

I knew Treasure's pain all too well. My pain was far much worse than this. I'm a 100% certain that what I endured with Goose was more than enough to drive any woman crazy. Shit, it pushed me to fake my death because I knew death was my only way out it, and Goose told me that on the daily. Starting over was the best thing I could have ever done, but that was a gift and a curse. I literally still live each day in fear of Goose. I worry that he will find me and really kill me, and I hated this fear shit with a passion.

I rubbed Treasure's back and decided to throw caution to the wind. I decided we needed to go out. I had to live my life, and that started today because Treasure needed to live too.

"Girl, fuck Shyne's cheating ass. Let's go out and enjoy Miami," I said, shocking her and my damn self.

"Oh my god, really? Little quiet Miss Sparkle is down to go out to the club and party?" Treasure shouted, hopping up from the couch, pulling me up with her and hugging me tightly.

"Let's go shopping, get our hair and nails done, and let's turn up tonight because come tomorrow, I will be apartment shopping and packing, and you can help me." Treasure rambled on nonstop, and I just laughed at her extra ass.

※

We got ready and hit the mall up where we shopped and pampered ourselves for hours before we finally left grabbing some Chick-fil-A on our way back to my apartment. By nine p.m., we were snapping pictures for Treasure's Snapchat, Facebook, and the gram. I didn't have any form of social media but after seeing the fun filters and all the cool features I was considering getting one for myself. We called up an Uber so that we could get lit tonight and not have to worry about driving. Treasure had access to all Shyne's cars, but we needed to drink dance and turn all the way up. We decided to hit up Club Luxe Grand. It was a nice upscale club that had one of the dopest DJs and two huge dancefloors on each level.

We were in our own VIP section just vibing drinking and doing our own thing. I was on cloud nine, having the time of my life with my best friend, and no one or anything could ruin that. I may have found our new past time for me and Treasure to let loose and be free.

I was on my third drink, and Treasure was probably on her fifth. She was standing up on the sofa in our section, winding her hips the Reggae beat, and I was seated sitting pretty dancing in my seat. I was just standing up when Treasure jumped down brushing past me fast damn near knocking me over and causing my drink to spill. I threw back the rest of my 1738 and followed behind the raging bull she had morphed into storming off through the crowd.

I rushed to catch up to her, but I wasn't fast enough because just as I reached her, she had thrown her drink in Shyne's face. We were diagonal across from our section in another larger section that Shyne was posted in standing off to the side with a chick in his lap the girl jumped up soaked from head to breasts in 1738, screaming and stomping like a child. Everything happened so fast from there that I didn't even see Shyne yoke Treasure up until he had her in the air by her neck.

I was trying my hardest to release Shyne's hand from around her throat. As I struggled to pry his hands-off Treasure, she kicked and clawed at him, drawing blood from his wrist. Security rushed up on us and helped separate everyone. Two guards pulled us one way, and one guard shoved Shyne the opposite direction towards the back of the club. The guards escorted us out the club and to the parking lot where they watched us as we waited on the Uber. Treasure was pissed off and had been going off the whole time we had been waiting for the Uber.

Although things ended abruptly, I still had a good time and an eventful night thanks to my front row seats at The Treasure and Shyne show. I was feeling good off the liquor and getting a kick out of Treasure still going off on a rant.

"What the hell are you smiling for Sparkle? This shit ain't even funny man. I'm so pissed right now!" she yelled and stomped her feet, crossing her arms over her chest, pulling me from my thoughts.

"Calm down, Mike Tyson. Just relax girl, damn. It's actually is hilarious. Treasure, sis, we gone laugh at this damn night one day soon, and then we'll be able to laugh about it forevvvva (in my Cardi B voice)," I said, laughing with tears just as the Uber pulled into the lot. Treasure rolled her eyes but burst out laughing right along with me.

Chapter Four

SHYNE

I was hot as fuck right about now behind Treasure's big head ass. This girl done came up in the VIP section I had for my team and some potential ruthless ass little niggas I needed as my hittas because they were official with their hit rate never missing a target. I was building my team up, and they were the missing piece I needed especially to show Honour that I should be the next distro for his new territory. I was trying to gain their respect and show them how good we were living over here to bait them into joining our team. This damn girl done showed her ass and showed out for real, and I was ready to smack her ass upside her head, but security saved her silly ass.

I had this sexy little Haitian chick I was trying to get to roll with me to the telly, but after Treasure ruined her dress and her made lace front lift, the bitch got ghost on a nigga. I had the right mind to head around to the front of the club and find Treasure so that I could smack some sense into her. I hadn't been home in a few days, and I wasn't taking her calls, but that doesn't matter. I'm the man of the house, and I do as I please. All she needs to do is sit pretty, spend my money, and take care of a nigga. Regardless of what I do, she supposed to act accordingly, carry herself better, and hold that shit down.

My side chick Rori was starting to take up all my time and juggling her with Treasure was becoming a task. Truth be told, I felt like ditching Treasure's ass and putting Rori in her spot. Rori had been around now for damn near a year, and I had no plans of letting her go. She had the best wet wet I've ever had, and her head was official.

I originally met Rori on some business shit, but she was feeling the kid from day one, and things started up and never stopped. Rori was a self-made boss, and the only female in Miami owning and operating a successful luxury car dealership. She was known to hook top dealers up with fly rides, but I had a business idea that proved to be lucrative for she and I, and we been rocking since then. Rori knew all about Treasure and made it a point to tell me to leave her alone and come be with her. I was really considering doing just that, but I felt obligated to Treasure since I moved her far away from her family and friends back home to follow my dope boy ambitions.

I came to Miami two years ago after my nigga Roman had to go take a time out and sit tight for a couple of years. He put me in contact with his people's Honour, the HNIC out here in Miami, and his reach went to damn near every state in the south. Roman told me if I wanted to make some real paper, then I needed to link up with Honour, put in that work, make them major moves, and I'd be straight.

I wasn't a true boss just yet, but I was damn near there, and I knew that once I secured the rest of my team, we would be so thorough that Honour would have no choice but to put me on and give me a higher position. The money was flowing in, everyone was eating, and all violators were always handled and checked immediately. I was able to provide and spoil Treasure. I had been slacking lately, but the truth is I loved Treasure, but I was feeling Rori too. The shit would be dope if they would agree to do the sister wives shit, but hey, I guess bitches had standards and shit or whatever.

I owed Treasure to take care of her and give her anything she wanted, and for a while, I did just that, but I'm a man, and Miami's got some bad females boy. Treasure had held shit down a few times when I was just nickel and diming and pushing real light work. She was down for me and loved me when I ain't have shit but a twin bed in my momma's basement. I knew I had to keep her when she followed me here. Shit, I had planned on marrying her ass and having a few babies but that all came to a standstill when Rori popped on the scene. I had two chicks that were willing to ride, and each gave me something the other couldn't.

Treasure was beautiful, but Rori was a bad chick. Rori reminded me of Jessica Dime from *Love & Hip Hop: Atlanta*. Rori was down for me and was a true team player. Treasure was always on me about leaving the game and starting a legit business. Treasure was ready for marriage and kids, and in the beginning, I wanted to give her just that, but Rori was down for the threesome party life and getting to the money. Rori was my Bonnie in the streets and a certified freak in the sheets. I knew sooner rather than later I'd either have to give them both an ultimatum just to deal how we are or let one go.

Somedays, Rori had me ready to drop Treasure, but then I remembered that she couldn't cook, and she doesn't clean shit she hires maids. That alone in my eyes was a red flag that she was not wife material and couldn't birth my kids at all. Treasure, on the other hand, was exactly that, the perfect wife and would be the perfect mother for my kids. She cooked, cleaned, and rubbed a nigga down at the end of the day, all that. However, lately, she be nagging me making me stay away from her because she was irritating. I know if I didn't get shit together, Treasure would pack up for sure and go back to Charlotte.

I left the club after smoking a few blunts to calm myself before I deal with Treasure. Tonight was perfect because Rori was in Vegas looking into expanding her dealership, so she should wouldn't be home until tomorrow. I knew Treasure was gone be on good bullshit once I got in the house, so I mentally prepared myself for a showdown, and then I'd dick her down properly like always. I'd maybe even put a seed up in her to keep her ass under lock and key. However, just before I had reached the exit for our condo off the highway, I had a picture message come in from Rori and that caused me to pass by my exit and keep going to hers.

Rori was back early and dressed in nothing but a thong and heels, and I wasn't passing her ass up now. I'd give Treasure a minute to cool off and head home in a few hours. I knew once I got in Rori's I'd have to power my phone up because Treasure was gone be blowing my line up.

I must have spoken too soon because the phone started to vibrate in the cup holder of my Range and the Media display said the incoming call was from Bossman A.K.A Honour. I knew already why he was calling, and he was probably pissed, so I let it roll to the voicemail. I know he got some shit to say about me pistol whooping Javier, but he crossed the line and was talking reckless, and I had to prove my point someway somehow. Right now, Rori was clouding my better judgment. Oh well, I'd hit him back later.

Chapter Five

HONOUR

I was laughing to myself to keep from spazzing out because this nigga had to take me for a damn joke. I was running out of patience for this nigga Shyne. I only looked out for him on the strength of my cousin Roman from Charlotte, NC. Roman was pushing heavy weight for me down there, and he said he wouldn't have been able to do it without his partner Shyne. Roman knows how I get down, so if I took on a referral that I didn't know personally, I must really respect, love, or fuck with you heavy.

When Roman took the plea deal on a bullshit gun charge, he sent Shyne my way. Now, in the beginning, he was on point and thorough. However, here we are two years later, and this nigga was feeling himself and was slacking with work. He was carrying on day to day like he was a boss out here making executive decisions without being given the directive to do so. I was calling this nigga for an emergency meeting because the pistol whooping that he decided to give Javier backfired on his ass in a major way.

Javier was so mad that he snatched up all the money, drugs, and guns from one of the top traps and was attempting to split town. He shot a little nigga in the leg that worked at the trap that tried to stop him before he dipped out of there.

I had my right hand goon ass little cousins Cairo and Pharaoh on his ass though. He thought he was about to get away, but they were waiting for the right time to snatch his ass up. Them little niggas loved the element of surprise when they had to put in work on some niggas or do a hit. This whole situation was all on Shyne, and this nigga had the nerve not to be answering the phone. I decided to go to his condo he thought I knew nothing about.

I hopped in my red McLaren 540c Coupe and hit the pedal to the metal over there. Twenty minutes tops and I was pulling into the parking lot of the Coral Gables Luxury Condos. I had a little cutie that stayed in these same condos, so I hit her up and asked her to let me in the building. She made me promise to stop up at her condo and see her once I finished whatever business I had to handle. I promised, but I never said tonight, and I guess she'd figure it out when I never showed up, but I didn't care. I was on a mission right now.

Once she buzzed me in the doors, I went right to the unit listing for mail to locate his unit number. I scanned over the mailbox directory until I came to Shyne's country bumpkin ass last name, Blumford with another name Belmont listed as well. I had no clue who name that was because his chick Rori had a big ass house somewhere far out, and her last name was Diaz. This nigga Shyne probably had a country ass chick up in this spot that he kept hidden from everyone. I wonder if Rori knew what this nigga was about, but knowing her she probably does know and just don't give a fuck. She's a shallow broad. Bad or not, she is weak as fuck.

I rode the elevator up to the sixth floor. I checked myself out on some G shit in the elevator mirrors cause a nigga was handsome, and I always stayed fresh as fuck. I was dressed real laid back and chill in my Nike jogger suit with the matching black Jordan retro 12's. As I was getting off and heading around the corner, I could hear a woman cursing loudly and going off. As soon as I turned the corner, my eyes fell upon a beautiful woman tossing clothes, I assume a nigga shit, out the door into the hall. I assumed she was the loud talker that I had heard when I first stepped off the elevator.

I checked my Bulova watch and realized it was well after four in the morning and was surprised that security hadn't been called yet on her. As I headed down the hall towards her, I realized that it was Shyne's apartment that she was going in and out of throwing clothes and items from. I walked right up to the door that had just closed behind her perfect round bottom in leggings and a sports bra. I waited off to the side after stepping over the mountain of items on the floor of the hallway. I could still hear her going off, but I didn't hear Shyne or anyone else saying anything.

She swung the door open and froze in place as our eyes met and locked in on each other. I was frozen speechless in my position against the wall posted up. I was captivated by this beauty, and her presence gave me a high.

"I'm sorry, can I help you with something?" she asked as she broke our intense stare and dropped the clothes into the pile.

"My bad, beautiful, I was looking for Shyne. Is he home?" I asked, never breaking eye contact with her. She huffed and rolled her eyes at the mention of his name, which made me smile.

"Fuck Shyne. He isn't here and as you can see, and he won't be here other than to pick this shit up!" she shouted as she did an about turn in her furry UGG house slippers and stormed back into the apartment.

I followed her inside and shut the door behind me. I observed the décor, and the place looked nice, but I could definitely tell a female decorated it. I walked into more shit scattered and thrown about around the apartment. She was nowhere to be found in the living room, so I assumed she had wandered to the back of the apartment. I had a seat at the bar and poured me a shot of D'usse. She stormed back out and screamed, grabbing her chest upon seeing me seated in her bar stools posted up with a shot that I went ahead and threw back. I winked at her and she rolled her eyes.

"Why are you all up in my house just helping yourself to whatever? That is just rude as fuck to invite yourself into someone's home, and you didn't even introduce your damn self," she said angrily with her hand propped up on her hip, and her other hand positioned as if to say *what the fuck?* like the memes that be going around. I couldn't help but laugh at her feisty little ass.

"My bad shorty, my name is Honour, and I'm Shyne's boss. It's imperative that I speak to him, so I decided to wait around," I replied as I stood to my feet and extended my hand to shake hers but was interrupted by the ringing of my cell phone.

Checking the caller ID, on the display, I saw that it was my cousin Pharaoh, my right hand calling me. I answered on the next ring right away to see what was good.

"Yo P, what's good?" I asked still watching lil mama watch me.

"Big cuz, we got a problem. Where are you at right now so I can come to you? This is major, and I don't usually do the whole emergency thing with you because I can handle shit on my own and you know that, but this shit is deep and requires your immediate attention boss man," he said, sounding defeated and worried, which caused me to be alarmed.

"Aight well I'm at Shyne's crib right now. I tried to pull up on him in person since he wasn't answering my calls and texts, but just his girl is here," I said, walking over to the bar to get another shot.

"Whoa nigga, you and shorty better get up outta there right now! We pulled the recording of Javier's car and he a rat nigga talking to the Feds as we speak and sending them Shyne's way. They are rounding up a team and coming to Shyne condo out in Coral Gables, so if that's the location you're at, I suggest you hightail it up outta there. You don't want none of the problems that they're about to bring Shyne way. Bro, dip now, I'm out." He disconnected the call, and I was stuck as to what the fuck was going on in my camp.

My first thought was just to dip out immediately, but I felt like I couldn't leave shorty here to be tied up in Shyne's mess.

"Yo, your man got the Feds hot on his trail. The Feds and S.W.A.T. will be coming here any minute, so I suggest you leave now like I'm about to do. If you need a ride, come on, shorty. Let me know where to take you. I'd feel better knowing you're not left behind and tied up in this shit," I said as I stood in the window and checked the parking lot.

"WHAT? OMG! I could kill this nigga. He fucking promised. Damn it! Treasure think... think. Shit, I don't have anyone other than my neighbor Sparkle, and I don't want to impose on her or wrap her in this shit either."

She was talking fast as she paced back and forth, running her hands through her hair.

"Baby girl, I know you don't know my rude ass at all, but I'ma be rolling out that door in the next minute, and if you are rolling, then let's go, but either way, I'm out," I said before heading towards the front door.

Once at the door I stopped and looked behind me to see her dash off to the back. I just shook my head as I went out the door assuming that she was staying put. All I could do was hope baby girl wasn't caught up in his mess.

"Hey, rude ass, wait up a damn minute. I didn't say I wasn't coming with you!" she yelled, running to catch up with me. She dragged her rolling luggage and a duffle bag over one shoulder and a purse in her other hand.

I just smiled at her as I held the elevator door open for her. Once on the elevator, we stood in silence. I was about to speak until the muffled barking noises erupted through the silenced elevator ride. I looked to her confused with a brow raised waiting for an explanation. She smiled back at me nervously and unzipped the duffle bag pulling out a fluffy white dog with big pink hair bows on each ear and a pink dog collar. All I could do was laugh and shake my head, grabbing her rolling luggage as we got off the elevator.

We headed through the lobby right out the front to my McLaren. I placed her bags in the trunk, and she sat holding her puppy in her lap in my front seat. I hopped in and started up the car, which had my music blasting immediately through the speakers. Future "March Madness" bumped loudly throughout as we pulled out the lot.

As we left the parking lot, a swarm of unmarked police cars was pulling up in the parking lot, and we both shook our heads in disbelief at how close we were to being right in the condo as they arrived. I don't know what I was thinking by snatching up and helping out Ms. Treasure, but I liked her presence and vibe right now, and she was having an effect on me.

I woke up to Cola licking my face and wagging her tail. It took me a minute to gather myself and remember where exactly I was. I remember the crazy situation at my condo that I almost got caught up in, and the thought had me pissed off all over again. We had just made it out of there when the Feds arrived in the parking lot, and I was just glad I had Honour to help me out. We shopped at Walmart for hours getting things for Cola and me because I only grabbed some basic things, but I needed my essentials. By the time we made it to Honour's place, we had gotten familiar with each other, and we ended up stayed up until almost nine this morning just talking and getting to know each other.

Honour was everything a woman could want and need in a real man. I was shocked that he was single with no kids, but he told me about how his ex-fiancée gave birth to a baby boy that turned out to not be his, so he has had trust issues since then. We talked about my situation and how I was going to handle leaving Shyne and living for me.

Honour offered to let me crash at his beautiful mini-mansion until I found myself a place. I appreciated the gesture, and I crashed last night, but I wasn't too sure if I'd stay longer than that. I was a bit thrown off at how comfortable and peaceful I felt around him though. I didn't feel this with Shyne, and we shared a home. In all honesty, our home hasn't ever been a home, but just somewhere we lived.

I checked my phone as I sat on the side of the king size bed. I had a few missed calls and text messages from Sparkle, so I shot her message explaining everything and told her I'd call her later. I handled my hygiene and threw on the plush robe hanging on the door of the bathroom.

I slipped on my furry UGG slippers and took Cola out through the sliding glass doors off the room that I was occupying. Cola roamed around sniffing about and finally settled by a nice palm tree to do her business. I left her to do her thing while I walked the fenced-in back-yard. He had a nice Olympic sized in-ground pool with a sectioned off Jacuzzi. There was a huge gazebo with a grill and bar built-in and even a hammock. I loved the flow of the backyard space. I took Cola back to the guest room where I poured her some food and water. I left Cola to eat and headed to wonder about the house just being nosey and admiring the beautiful home décor.

I eventually stumbled upon a gym in the back of the house where I could hear Future's "Stick Talk" blasting through the room. I peeked in the crack of the door and a lump formed in my throat at the sight of a shirtless and sweaty Honour doing pull-ups on some bar contraption. His glistening abs and biceps were chiseled to perfection. I was getting a little worked up and excited watching him work out, causing blood to rush to regions unknown and forgotten to me and my so-called man Shyne for the last few months. I did a quick turn and headed back to the guest room before Honour saw my creep ass eyeing him up. I tripped over a sneaky Cola and fell flat on my face with the robe up, exposing my bare rear end.

I was stuck in place trying to get up before Honour came out and saw me, but my knee was burning and hurting, along with my wrist. I wasn't quick enough because he was in the hall rushing to help me up. He had a gun in his hand that he placed in the small of his back before bending down to help me up. We briefly laughed before he asked if I wanted to join him for brunch in about two hours on a yacht. I accepted the invite and went to get ready. After my shower, I took the time to block Shyne because he had been sending me crazy messages and calling more than he had in our last year together.

First, he started all concerned and worried, especially when he was made aware that the Feds came to the condo looking for him. I guess he thought they took me in, but after checking into whether I was in police custody and finding that I wasn't, he threatened for me to call him asap and to bring my short ass home. I wasn't paying Shyne no type of attention though he would get the picture soon enough that I was done with his ass.

I moisturized my skin from head to toe and wore my silk pressed hair with a part down the middle. I dressed in a summer floral maxi dress, Tory Burch thong sandals to match, and a pink Kate Spade bag.

I went in search of Honour through the home and finally found him in his den at the bar sipping a drink with a cigar in his hand. He was dressed casually in a pair of khaki shorts, a fresh white Lacoste polo, and some white Air Force Nike Ones. His Cuban link chain glistened as the sunlight from the nearby window shined on it. His waves were spinning, and his edge up was sharp and on point. He looked so much like the rapper Nelly that they were damn near almost twins. He winked at me, causing me to blush. He was seriously one of the sexiest men I had ever seen, and in Miami, fine ass men were everywhere, but he was taking first place in my opinion.

He stood to greet and hug me, and the YSL cologne that invaded my nose was mesmerizing. I hadn't known this man for more than twenty-four hours, and he had me feeling things I never expected in such a short time. The level of comfort that I felt was mind-blowing to me, but I wasn't backing down from this quality time he was offering. I'd sit and talk or ride around doing nothing with him all day any day. He handled me so gently and delicately like he really valued me and yet he barely knew me. I was in the presence of a real man and a true boss. He spoke to me as if I was his lady and not the ex-girlfriend of his business associate.

"You said you have a friend you hang with, right? Well, is she single and down to hang out with us today?" he asked before finishing off his drink and placing the glass on the bar.

"My best friend's name is Sparkle, and yea, she should be down to hang. Do you got somebody for her? She needs to get out. She never does anything besides hang with me and still does nothing. Give me one second to text her," I said while I immediately started to text Sparkle.

Sparkle took a little convincing but finally agreed to meet us at the pier. Honour decided to drive us there in his McLaren again, and the car was bad. We laughed, talked, and vibed the whole ride there. I had been honest with him about my relationship with Shyne or the lack thereof. He opened up some more to me about his ex-girl, Tuesday.

Once we got that out the way and we were on the same page as far as what the other wanted out of a friendship to start things were good. I had mentioned how I needed to start looking right away for a place and a car. He said he had a realtor and a friend who owned a dealership, so he would link me with them. He asked me one question that stuck out to me and was weighing on me a little bit, which was what do I want to do now that I had my life back and no longer was living for and how Shyne wanted me to. I was quiet as I thought of what I truly wanted, and then it hit me.

"I would love to open a restaurant. I went to culinary school and was in the top of the class when I graduated but put all that on hold to follow Shyne here and play housewife. However, I am now going to focus on that." I smiled as he smiled back at me, and then I looked out the window feeling good about the decisions I made.

"Baby girl, you will do just that and more. I'm a make sure of that, and that's a promise," he said, winking at me as he whipped the car into a parking spot.

He opened my door and grabbed my hand, helping me out of the passenger seat. He locked his fingers into mine, leading me up the dock to the yacht. Once we stepped onto the yacht, we were led to the upper level that had a breathtaking view. I was handed a glass of wine and stood at the rail overlooking the water. Honour excused himself while he headed to the group of men at the other end of the top level.

I sipped my drink and enjoyed the scenery loving how at peace I felt just in a matter of hours compared to how stressed I was these last few months with Shyne. I had cried my last tears and stressed for the last time that was for sure. Regardless of if I met Honour or not, that was my plan. Honour and his presence was the cherry on top.

I heard my name being called in the distance behind me. I turned to see Sparkle waving to me as she walked through the parking lot towards the dock. She made her way over to the dock and climbed aboard the yacht, looking flawless as always. Sparkle was brown skin and petite, but she had curves that filled out her shape and fit her body perfectly. She wore her natural hair in a long wrap style parted on the right side. She was dressed in a cute hot pink romper short set with some nude wedge sandals with a matching hat and bag. I was still so confused why Sparkle was single because she was effortlessly flawless.

I watched as the guys, including Honour's friends, watched her come aboard the yacht and prance right on over to me, and we hugged. I flagged the waiter carrying the champagne over to get Sparkle a glass. Once she had her glass, we headed back to the balcony to chat.

"Girl, which one is the friend because they all are fine," she voiced lowly while sipping her champagne and eyeing the guys.

"I'm not sure. I think they are talking business right now, so we will have to wait for them to finish up and come over here to find out," I said, sipping from my glass and waving to Honour who had just winked at me.

"What the hell have I missed in the last forty-eight hours of us being dragged out of the club to now because you two are giving off some real vibes right now and the googly eyes are something serious."

Sparkle laughed at me as I rolled my eyes at her observant ass. I finally broke the intense gaze I was locked in with Honour and gave Sparkle my undivided attention.

"I don't know Sparkle. We've been vibing, but I just left Shyne, so I'm not trying to take things to that level, but everything is flowing on its own effortlessly. I can't lie. I like it, and I like being around him. I feel so comfortable. Anyways, I blocked Shyne, and I will get my things one of these days. I will be moving real soon because Honour has some real estate people for me to meet," I said before finishing off my drink.

"He is too fine Treasure, and he keeps watching you girl he is feeling you for real for real" Sparkle said smiling before high fiving me like some schoolgirls with some good gossip.

"I think I'm feeling him too, honestly. I'm just nervous and don't want to play no games at all, but I guess I'll see where this goes. It's so weird girl because we have this strong ass connection," I said as we watched Honour and a shorter guy with dreads headed over towards us.

My heart started to race the closer Honour got towards me,. I felt like I've known this man longer than twenty-four hours. The conversations and the way he treated me it all had me on cloud nine.

As soon as they were upon us, Honour introduced us both to his cousin Pharaoh, who was eyeing Sparkle and giving her his undivided attention. We could tell that the feeling was mutual because Sparkle was blushing and widely smiling as they talked. He grabbed her hand and led her below deck to talk in a more private setting.

Honour led me to a table not too far in the back of the upper deck not too far away from being able to see them over the rail looking down on the second level. We ate some shrimp cocktail appetizers as we waited for the meal to be served. I was starting to feel a buzz and decided to stand and try to let the air sober me up. As soon as I stood and looked out over the railing Beyoncé and Jay-z "Boss" came on. I started to dance and sway my hips.

I looked back over my shoulder making eye contact with Honour, who was smiling watching me dance. He finally stood and came over to join me in my dancing. We slowed danced with my rear pushed into him, and his arms wrapped around my waist. I could stay this way with him all day.

"What you know about being with a boss?" he whispered in my ear, causing me to become warm and tingly all over.

"To keep it a buck with you I honestly don't know much about dating a boss, but I know how to treat my man when I have one," I said, trying to sound confident and not like the nervous wreck that I was.

"You stick with me, and you'll see exactly what being with a boss is like. I can show you better than I can tell you beautiful," he said, speaking with so much conviction before kissing my neck softly. I didn't utter a word because I honestly was speechless. I just closed my eyes and enjoyed the vibe. If being with a Boss was anything like this then I may just stick around.

Chapter Seven

PHARAOH

A nigga done had some fine ass women, but none and I do mean none of them have ever been as fine as this chocolate beauty next to me. When my big cuz Honour said he had a girl for me to meet, I was expecting another water head, birdbrain groupie looking for a come up. The ones wanting to be taken care of and trap a nigga with a baby so that they could benefit from it. I was never expecting to be interested and entertaining the idea of really getting to know her. I wanted to know all about Sparkle Reynolds.

The laugh she released was like a bolt of electricity through my body. The conversation was effortless and flowed so well between us that I didn't realize that the sun was going down, and we were approaching the docks again. The vibe and the way she carried herself was intoxicating and I liked it surprisingly.

I didn't want the date to end, so I asked Sparkle out for a game of pool and drinks. Shit, at this point, I'd walk the beach holding hands discussing dreams of rainbows and unicorns and all that other girly shit just to be around her. Sparkle was reserved and wasn't trying to open up too much, but my ass was talking a mile a minute like a little kid with a crush. I had planned to get through the wall she had up and get to know the real woman behind it. There was a story there that I wanted to know. We all headed to the pool hall where we all hung out until damn near three in the morning. I hadn't spent quality time with a woman in years outside of getting some cutty and even then, I wasn't kicking it I was in and out after I got my nut.

Sparkle promised to text me in the morning so that we could set up a date asap. I had some shit I had to handle at the traps, so I headed there first. Once I was done making my rounds and making sure everything was everything, I was ready to go home and call it a night. We all rotated weeks for collecting money and distributing the product. I was gone get some real sleep and try to spend my weekend with Sparkle.

I sent my brother Cairo a text letting him know the new code to the safes before powering my trap cell off. Swapping codes was something we implemented to ensure that no one was able to find it out except Honour, Cairo, and me, and we changed them at the end of each week before we switched. I rode home with the music on, but Sparkle was heavy on my mind the whole time. This girl had me open already and still didn't know too much about her.

I arrived at my townhome rather quick, not playing at all because the twenty-four hours with no sleep was starting to catch up to me. I parked in my assigned parking space and turned the car off. I sat for a minute talking myself into getting out; that's how tired I was. I hopped out and headed up the walkway to my home. I fumbled the keys around looking for my house key when some rustling in the bushes startled me.

I pulled my strap out and cocked it back ready to shoot first and ask questions never, but a black cat scurried across my path, causing me to relax some. I was about to put my strap back in my waist when I was met with a devious smile. As soon as I turned around, I stood in the face of my ex-girl Armani. Armani stood on my porch steps in her ratchet girl stance, hand on her hip with her left foot cocked out like a damn pigeon or something. She had this big ass goofy smile once we had been staring at each other for a few minutes like I would be happy to see her snitching ass. I was annoyed that quick by her presence, and my high from the day was blown.

I decided to go around her and just ignore her before things got ugly between us like they usually did. I was tired and wasn't about to play the games tonight with Armani because after the stunt she pulled on me a few months ago, I'll fuck around and really hurt her ass tonight. I honestly owe her an ass whooping for the way she fucked my car up two weeks ago, but I was gone let her make it tonight and keep it pushing on in the house.

I brushed past her and unlocked my door. I was almost done pushing the door closed all the way when she put her big ass foot in the door stopping it. I started to slam the door shut on her foot, but she'd just call the cops on a nigga like she did lying on me last time.

"Wait, Pharaoh, let me in?" she shouted through the opening in the door.

"Why the hell are you here, Armani?" I yelled, sticking my face in the opening of the door looking at her trying to push the door open, but it was pointless because it was no way in hell that she was bringing her ass up in here.

"Nigga, open this damn door and quit playing with me! You got these neighbors looking out the window at me and shit like I'm crazy!" she screamed, trying to push the door off her foot that was starting to get squished.

"Shit, yo ass is crazy! What the fuck you mean? Armani, you got two minutes before I break your damn foot because I'm getting this door shut regardless. Your ass be looking like the wicked witch of the west when that house fell on her ass around this bitch, keep playing with me," I replied, still applying my weight on the door to keep her ass out.

"Oh, so it's like that? You're acting brand new on me now?" she yelled, rolling her eyes and smacking her lips.

"Hell, yeah it's like that. I'm trying really hard not to smack fire from your hard of hearing ass, but you're not making that shit easy. The last encounter we had you got my ass locked up for some bogus ass breaking and entering knowing damn well you locked my ass out of the condo we shared, and I paid for. I let you get away with that dumb shit and gave your ass the car and condo, yet instead of being appreciative that, you're still alive and kicking because me being who the fuck I am. I could have left yo ass floating with fish. But no, you here starting up some unnecessary bullshit, so we ain't got shit to talk about.

Armani, go on somewhere with that shit, move the fuck around before shit gets real!" I stressed to her beyond aggravated at this point.

"I said I was sorry about that. It's been almost two months, Pharaoh. Damn, let it go. We always get back. What's different now? I know you miss me, so let me come in and make it up to you," she said, trying to use her sex appeal to persuade me.

I smirked, and she thought she had me, so she pulled her foot out and bent down to pick up her bags, and as soon as I saw her do that, I slammed the door shut locked it and put my alarm on. At one point in life, I used to fall for Armani schemes, but once I caught her ass on the phone telling my moves and plans to her brother, I knew she couldn't be trusted. See, Armani thought I didn't know she was a scam artist, but I knew and never let her know that I had discovered it.

Once she got me arrested for breaking in her our condo, I let her ass go. See, I could have hurt her shit, and I could have killed her and her brother, but completely cutting her off was way better. Since we now had documented domestic disputes, I couldn't end her ass, but I had stripped everything from her except the car and condo, which was bought and paid for, so she should consider herself lucky.

I could hear her cursing me smooth out, but I ain't give not one flying fuck. She started banging on my door, and I knew sooner or later the neighbors were gone report her ass, so I kept it pushing upstairs to my master suite to shower and sleep so that I could dream about Sparkle's fine ass.

Chapter Eight

SHYNE

I can't believe this nigga Javier ratted me out to the damn Feds. The Feds came in and tore my condo apart, taking whatever the hell they wanted mostly materialistic shit. They left me a confiscation list taped on my door along with a business card for a Detective Willmore with a request to give him a call as soon as possible. I wasn't speaking to them pigs though. They could forget that. If they had any actual evidence, they would be issuing a warrant for my arrest. I would hit my lawyer up and see if they even had proper papers to enter my home and take my shit.

I'd been home for a day now and couldn't find Treasure's dumb ass, and she had my number blocked. After the mess that happened at the club, I figured I'd let her cool off, but she clearly wasn't over that shit yet.

Rori was on my case about being exclusive and tired of being a side chick, and that shit was starting to stress my ass out. Once she started that shit, I waited until she was in the shower, and I dipped out, blocking her number until I could handle shit with Treasure. I never expected to walk into this shit with the Feds. I had Honour blowing my line up, and I needed to go check in with him and see what he was on after this bullshit with Javier. I left Treasure damn near fifty text messages, and she still ain't hit me back. I needed to get my bitch in line and back home before she decides to take flight and leave my ass for good this time.

I knew she'd be pissed off with me, but usually, I sweet talk my way out of it by apologizing then take her shopping and spend a few days in the house with her to be back in her good graces. My gut was telling me this time though shit was different, and I may have played with her for the last time. She has never stayed out away from our home, and she has never blocked my calls in our whole five years. I usually had to ignore her back-to-back calls when some shit happens with a chick I'm sliding out with on her, but not this time around, and that had all the red flags going up in my mind.

I decided to check across the hall and see if Sparkle had seen her or at least heard from her. I could hear someone singing inside the unit and heard things moving around as I listened at the door. I knocked and waited for her to answer the door. The door cracked open, Sparkle stuck her face out, and upon seeing me, she rolled her eyes at me.

"Tuhhh, what do you want, Shyne?" she asked with attitude dripping all in her voice.

"Yo, you can chill with the attitude alright. I ain't in the mood for that shit. All I came over here for was to see if your lonely, miserable ass was hiding Treasure in there, or if you knew where she was so that I can bring her ass home. I'm sick of playing this hide and seek game with her," I said irritated as hell with this whole situation.

"Nigga, don't come to my door with that shit. Frankly, my dear, I don't give a fuck what you're not in the mood for. I ain't seen her or talked to her, and even if I had, I would never tell your tired ass no way. Get the hell away from door clown!" she yelled and then slammed the door in my face.

I know her dumb ass was lying for Treasure, but it was all good. I let her have that slick shit she just pulled talking reckless like I wouldn't slap her ass smooth across her face. I decided to let this shit blow over while I handled some business because I was sure Treasure would be home eventually.

I was stressed and decided to slide over to Rori's place and kick it. Hopefully, she'd calmed down, and I'd give her some attention until I caught up with Treasure. I bent a few corners and hit some traps before turning my phones off for the day. I was going off the grid for a week to get me a mental break, and some good sex was in order too.

Rori was gone accept me with open arms, especially since I'd be able to lay up with her for a whole week. Maybe making Rori my main bitch wasn't such a bad idea after all. Nahhhh, who was I kidding. She was a good lay and cool company, but she wasn't wife material. She couldn't even cook Ramen noodles right. She paid people to clean, and she refused to stop hustling and being on the scene every damn weekend. I needed my bitch to be able to cook, clean, and raise my kids. My future wife needed to keep her ass at home while I make moves and take care of them. Therefore, I needed Treasure back she was already trained and submissive to what I wanted and needed. I'd give her ass one more week on this hiatus before I kicked up my tactics at getting her home.

Chapter Nine

HONOUR

Two Weeks Later

I finally caught up with Shyne after all these weeks of trying to reach his ass. I was strolling the mall with Pharaoh and as we waited for the ladies to finish shopping. Treasure was still around, but she was considering moving in with Sparkle into a condo not far from me. Treasure and Sparkle had been cool as hell to kick it with, and we all had been kicking it heavy since I walked in Treasure's house. We had done a few double dates, and now the ladies wanted to shop for our trip to Punta Cana. We always took a guys trip once a year, but since the ladies were around, we invited them to tag along on an all-expense paid trip.

We had just left the girls at Macy's while we headed to the Gucci store. As soon as we walked into the store, we spotted Shyne and Rori trying on matching Gucci sneakers. I was getting a kick out of this because he was begging and damn near crying for Treasure to come home just this morning. We had listened to all the voicemails he had left her and read all the text messages just last night of him begging her to come home, but this what type of shit he was on today. This nigga was such a clown, and he hadn't even realized how quick we snatched back his traps from him. He called himself putting his mans Rell in charge while he took some time off.

Little did he know Rell was now in charge and reporting to us. His ass was no longer getting money with us. He was sloppy, lazy, and a flight risk, so instead of taking any chances, he was removed. He still owed me some bread, and I was just gone tell his ass as a parting gift to keep that shit. He was laughing and kissing all up on Rori when we strolled right over interrupting, they little Bey and Jay moment. He looked like he saw a ghost once he laid eyes on us posted up around them by the mirrors in the back of the store.

I watched as Shyne scrambled to his feet to try and speak to us, but I threw my hand up stopping him before he could even get a word out because I didn't want to hear whatever he was about to say at this point. I just observed while mean mugging him as he tried to stand up tall and put on this front for Rori. Shyne was clearly mistaken if he thought he even was a factor right now to her with my presence here. Rori's been on my dick for years on in now, and I always curved her trick ass.

His little tough act meant nothing right now because I could take Rori at this moment and he wouldn't be able to do shit about. She'd jump at the chance to go too. I guarantee it. However, she wasn't the prize at all, and his goofy ass didn't even know it. Treasure was the prize, and that's who I had my eyes set on.

"Shyne, Shyne, Shyne, ummph, umph, umph. So, you thought it was smart to duck and dodge me while the Feds is hot on your trail and done rolled through your spot thanks to Javier who you couldn't keep in line from the jump and failed to recognize he was an opp that turned on you?" I spoke through clenched teeth because I was trying to remain calm, but seeing him was making it hard.

"Nah, Honour, big homie. It's not even like that. I've just been lying low, and I already hit up my lawyer, and he's on top of it the shit with the Feds and..."

He was rambling fast and stumbling over his words, sounding guilty as hell, so I threw my hand up again to stop him from talking. I laughed to myself, and Pharaoh laughed as well while shaking his head at this clown.

"I tell you what Shyne, take all the time you need to lay low because your services are no longer needed this way. You are no longer getting money with this team. Your territory and runners already started reporting to Rell yesterday. That bread you owe me and that product you got left, take that as a parting gift my nigga."

I watched as his eyes got big as saucers, and his mouth hung open in shock. Rori was behind him looking pissed, biting her bottom lip like she was anxious to say or do something, but baby girl knew better than to fuck with me, so she remained silent.

"You slipped across each board, man, better luck next time. The good thing is there ain't no repercussions behind your fuck ups. There's no need for me to do anything to you because you did it all to yourself on your own. I looked you out on the strength of Roman, but you dropped the ball and your most prized possession. You know what they say, one man's trash is another man's *Treasure*!" I spoke sternly to him, and then for the hell of it, I emphasize Treasure's name.

He looked confused as hell until I think it finally all clicked when he looked me square in the eye and his jaw clenched tight, the vein protruded in his forehead, and his fist balled as tight as Arthur's did on the viral meme. I just smirked and strolled my ass on up out of there to go get my Treasure.

Chapter Ten

GOOSE

O n July 11th, 2017, my life turned upside down. The day that my wife died sent me on a downward spiral. I have been sick since the day Crystal was killed in the car crash. We had to have a closed casket because of how badly that she was burned up, and after the services, I got her body cremated. I was only able to identify her body from the jewelry she wore and her burned up work badge. My mind is consumed with her and how wrong I did her. I kiss her urn each morning and at night. I've barely slept since she's been gone, and guilt ate at me every single day. I did a lot of fucked up shit to her, but I never wanted her to be gone from me forever.

They say to give the woman and ones you love the flowers while they are here and that was so true to me now. My dad Duck brought me up. He was a ruthless ass pimp in the 80s until the late 90s, and he raised me the pimp way. His motto was to keep your woman and hoes in line by choice or by force. Nine times out of ten, he had to lay down the law by force, and that's all I knew.

Nevertheless, as I reflect now, I realize how wrong that shit is. Well, I guess hindsight is 20/20. I always dabbled in weed laced with coke and pills, but recently I had picked up more of a straight coke habit over the other vices now that Crystal was gone. My life was a living hell and a wreck. I was sitting in the same spot for three days now getting high. I dragged my ass to the bathroom and just stared at myself in the mirror. From outside looking in, no one could tell I had a habit. I still was a fly nigga. I showered and decided to check on my hoes and collect my money. I took over for my father, and my brother Bird ran the chop shops and check cashing places. I checked the piled up mail and tossed everything on the couch. On my way out the house, a letter addressed to Crystal stood out.

I opened the letter, and it was an invitation to participate in a survey about the ordering of the lifelike dolls she had purchased. I was so confused, but I decided to sit my ass at her laptop that was still in its original place at her desk in our spare room. I went on the website and typed in the company's URL. I searched the orders by her order number from the notice. I was shocked and confused when I saw two custom lifelike adult dolls that were ordered two weeks before Crystal died almost two years ago. This was all weird, but I was gone get some answers on what this was all about.

I decided I needed to call in a favor from this private investigator that I knew who owed me a favor for some work I put in for him a few years ago. I was tripping because the reviews on the lifelike dolls said it's hard to know if it's fake at first before inspection. It was something real sketchy going on, and I was gone get to the bottom of it. This shit was weird as hell and had me questioning if I was losing my damn mind? Right about now, that is how I was feeling.

I finally had more info from my PI after about three weeks of waiting, and according to him, it appears that the crash investigation was closed and was no way to get more information. Crystal's body was cremated, so it's no way for me to know if the doll was used, but my gut was telling me that she faked her death on me. I used to always wonder why she liked watching those movies where the woman escaped and changed her identity or faked her death, and now, I think that's exactly what her ass did. The PI was able to hack into the phone system for AT&T where her old iPhone was purchased through.

In the web browsing history, he located multiple searches on identity changing and ticket information on Charlotte, NC. We searched for weeks there, and I even hit up some old friends of ours who didn't know anything, but my one of homeboy said he swears he had seen a girl that looked just like Crystal working at the hospital. I had the PI check into it, but no record of a Crystal Rowe existed. He had a connect in the hospital that he sent pictures to and we were waiting to see if they could match it to anyone in the employee database. I decided to check on Crystal's family home in Savannah to see if she'd been there. It sounded crazy, but I knew her ass was alive somewhere, and I was going to find her.

&a.

I arrived at the countryside home and noticed nothing out of place from when I was last here three years ago with Crystal. I still paid a service to keep up the house and take care of the yard as we had done when she was alive. It was worth a lot of money, and I had no access to the deed to sell it now that Crystal had passed, hmmph "supposedly passed away". I'd been getting pissed day by day at the fact that I mourned her and felt guilty for how I treated her, and now she had played me all along. Well now, I plan to get my hands on her and wring her fucking neck. Since she wants to play dead and disappear, now I'd make her wish come true.

I entered the home from the front of the house. The house sat on I don't even know how many acres and had a huge wrap around porch. With five bedrooms, three baths, and an in-law- suite, the home was worth almost one million. The land was inherited and passed down from many generations, but I didn't give a fuck about that. I really wanted to sell this shit for the money. Something stood out to me now upon walking into the family room. I immediately noticed a blanket on the rocking chair folded up.

The blanket wouldn't have bothered me much had it not been Crystal's favorite PINK plush blanket from a few birthdays ago that she got after we spent damn near $200 on panties on sale. The blanket was free, but she loved it and always snuggled up with it. That was all the confirmation that I needed that she was here since her "passing". Damn, she was legit out in this world alive somewhere starting a new life without me. She probably ran off with some nigga and played my ass. I couldn't wait to catch up to her because I owed her payback for all the days I cried and blamed myself for her death, a death that never happened. Nevertheless, I guess this was just practice for the slow death that I was bringing upon her.

Chapter Eleven
SPARKLE

These last few weeks that I had spent with Pharaoh had been beyond amazing and some of the best times that I've had in a very long time. I loved the way we had fun together and how we could talk to each other about anything. Just last night as we talked about our childhood and into who we were now, I felt so comfortable that I had almost come clean about who I truly was and how I ended up in Miami as a girl name Sparkle.

Outside of my name, everything about me was real. I was being my authentic self with him. He knew my name as Sparkle Reynolds, but he was seeing the real me, Crystal Rowe. Pharaoh was my homie first, and that gave us a solid foundation for when we became lovers, which I knew we would be that by the end of this trip, if not by tonight, the first night in Punta Cana. We flirted all day and night whether face to face, via text message, or FaceTime, and we laughed and constantly joked, ribbing and roasting each other.

Pharaoh didn't mind spending time with me indoors in the comfort of our homes. He was cool with me being a homebody, and I appreciated that so much. Lately, he has been able to convince me to get out and do more, and I loved it, especially if it was with him or Treasure. I knew that after four weeks into this that I was most definitely falling in love with him. It happened fast, but it occurred so effortlessly that I didn't realize it until I found myself not wanting to be apart from him for too long.

What we shared was everything that my relationship with Goose wasn't. He did everything Goose refused, and he didn't treat me as if he owned, but instead, like he never wanted to lose me. I was valuable and felt adored, and for me, that was so out of the ordinary that I was scared shitless that something was about to come our way and destroy whatever we were creating.

In my heart, I knew Pharaoh was the one for me. After all this time, he gave me back that hopeless romantic feeling I'd long lost as a teen. My heart was locked and ready, but it was my mind and my paranoia that was causing me to question how long we'd have. Was I too damaged and broken to give him all of me as he is willing to give me all of him? I had so many doubts and concerns, and the feeling in the pit of my stomach told me something was about to crash our world.

Today we were flying out to Punta Cana, and I was so excited that I decided to ignore the feeling I was having of trouble on the horizon. I had stayed the night with Pharaoh this whole week, and I loved every minute of it.

I used the guest bathroom to get some privacy and let Pharaoh get ready in his room. As I stepped out of the shower, I realized I left my towel and moisturizer in the room. I dashed out the guest bathroom trying to get to his master bedroom, hoping that he was already in the shower. I tiptoed down the hall and into the bedroom, and just as I was grabbing the towel, I was startled by a gasp and the sound of glass crashing against the floor. I jumped dropping the towel and turning to see what the noise was.

I could see a bottle of aftershave had broken on the floor. Pharaoh stood there in the doorway of his bathroom wrapped in his towel eyeing me lustfully and holding onto the monster covered behind his towel with his lower lipped tucked tightly between his teeth. I quickly reached for the towel, grabbing it in my hands trying to hide my naked body, but I never got the chance to wrap myself in it because Pharaoh was on me so fast. I was tired of the pent up sexual tension between us, so I threw caution to the wind dropping the towel once again, and I wrapped my arms around his neck as he lifted me, wrapping my legs around his waist. We kissed with so much hunger and passion for each other that I felt the heat rise in the room. I needed and wanted this bad.

Pharaoh laid me down on the bed as he removed his towel and pulled a condom out his top nightstand drawer. I refused to look, but my curiosity got the best of me, and my eyes traveled down his chiseled chest to his strong arms. As he rolled the condom down onto his erect shaft, I let out a gasp of my own this time once my eyes focused on the girth and length of his dick. It had been some years for me since my last sexual encounter, so I was more than ready to feel him inside me. However, I'd be lying if I said I wasn't scared for the pain that I was sure would come. He took no time throwing my legs on his shoulders and diving in face first to my dripping honeypot. He was not shy and didn't hold back as he tasted my juices that flowed freely.

I felt like I was having an out of body experience as the pleasure took over me and gave me the euphoric feeling I'd yearned for. I felt my orgasm building up, and he took no mercy on me as he gave me a tongue lashing that would go down in history for me as the most satisfying and erotic feeling I have ever felt. I tried to stifle the moans, but it was no luck. Before I knew it, I was releasing a flood onto his sheets and screaming to anyone that could hear.

As I came down off that high, basking in the feeling with my eyes closed just enjoying the after effect, I was jolted out that trance when I felt the head of his member trying to push its way into my folds. I stared into his eyes, and although I saw the lust, my heart felt the love. I couldn't speak any audible words as he inched further into me. I dug my nails into his back as he placed kisses along my neck and breasts. With one final thrust, he was completely in where he just sat savoring our first encounter. He began to stroke in and out of me sending me clawing more at his back as I felt the pleasure of the strokes that he gave to me. Pharaoh was making love to me, and I felt that in my soul. I was on the verge of another orgasm causing the heat to rise again between us. Pharaoh picked up the pace, and we kissed tongues exploring as we both erupted in an intense orgasm that shook the headboard. I hope his neighbors weren't home.

Chapter Twelve

HONOUR

I had everything ready for the trip and was on my way out the door to load the car up with our bags so that we could head to the airport. I opened the door and was met with a familiar but unexpected face. My ex-girl Tuesday stood on my porch staring at me with those hazel eyes that used to draw me in. I'd be a lying ass nigga if I said that she didn't look good. She had that perfect hourglass shape, the one my money paid Dr. Miami, the best in the city, to sculpt it to perfection. I instantly grew mad as I thought of the reason we were no longer together. Tuesday chose her body, looks, and becoming an Instagram model and video chick over carrying our baby.

"Tuesday, why are here? Yo, now is not a good time," I spoke inches from her face with clenched teeth. It was taking everything in me not to drag her ass after I told her to never let me see her face again.

"Well, hello to you too Honour. Long time no see. Are you heading somewhere?" she said, peeking over my shoulder looking into the entryway.

I just shook my head and pulled the door closed behind me as I stepped out further onto the porch. The last thing I wanted to do was mess up with Treasure before we even got started.

"I don't know why you are here Tuesday, and I don't care for real, so please get from around here. I warned you not to bring your ass back around here when you killed my baby, and I guess you take my threats lightly." I stepped in her face, and she jumped back, almost falling down catching herself on the railing.

"Honour, this is how you gone treat me after everything we been through? I know it's because of that *bitch* in there. I saw her nosey ass looking over the railing upstairs in your house!" she yelled, stomping her feet in place like a toddler about to throw a fit.

I was disgusted looking at her, and she was pushing my buttons, so I breathed in and out counting to ten and walked around her to the Hummer truck I had pulled out and parked in the driveway for us to ride to the airport in. I felt Tuesday behind me as I loaded the luggage in the truck, and I decided to ignore her until she got the hint and left.

"You know what Honour, fuck you! I came here to clear the air and apologize, but to also let you know about some shit I overheard, but it's all good you figure it out on your own!" she yelled and then she stomped all the way to her blue Mustang that I had purchased her a few years ago and sped off.

I was left wondering what she was talking about, but I ain't have time for all that. Knowing her, it was just some bullshit ass gossip. I rushed inside to let Treasure know we were all set to roll out. I entered the house, and it was quiet, which was odd because Treasure had a 90s playlist on earlier that she was jamming to as she got ready and sipped on her champagne.

I searched all over the lower level, not finding her anywhere, so then I headed upstairs. I checked the messages that came in on my cell as I entered my bedroom and it was Pharaoh letting me know he was on his way to the private jet and that he had copped a few bottles to pop on the plane. I shot him a quick text letting him know that we would be leaving out right now as well. When I entered the room, Treasure was dressed in a pair of skinny jeans, a white crop top, and fresh white Air max 95's. I admired her from behind as she put her earrings on in the floor length mirror. She winked at me in the mirror as I came upon her and placed my hands around her waist, resting my nose in the crook of her neck.

She smelled good in the YSL Mon Paris that I had picked up for her a few days ago. I wanted Treasure in the worst way, but she was holding out on a nigga tough. We almost took it there last night after the drinks and chilling in the Jacuzzi, but as soon as I had her cornered and pulled into me close so that she could feel how brick my shit was in the boxer briefs that I wore my business phone rang, and I had to make an important run. By the time I got back home, she was in a damn onesie pajama set knocked out in the guest room. I was on straight bullshit once we got to the DR. I was pulling all the stops to get her, but the thing was I wanted to keep her. This wasn't a one-time thing. Treasure was the type of chick that I wanted to have my kids and be the woman of this castle greeting me every night when I make it home.

We hurried out the house to the car and hopped in wasting no time burning rubber to the private jet. I played Usher and Zaytoven's new EP "A" and was surprised to see Treasure was rocking to it too. I took her as the Beyhive only type, but shorty was feeling the songs. We arrived at the parking garage for long term parking. Once parked, we grabbed a trolly cart to pull our bags to the private jet hanger. Sparkle ran right to Treasure upon seeing us on the walkway. Pharaoh pulled out all the stops with a red carpet and multiple flight attendants. I knew this trip was about to be one to remember.

I hadn't taken a trip, let alone one with a female in a long time. I was looking forward to enjoying my time with Treasure and getting to know everything about her. I wasn't pressed for no females. They came a dime a dozen, but the hold Treasure had on me was the force driving me to pursue her so heavily right now. When I was around her, she made me feel good, but she made me want to do and be good, and that is what really sealed it for me. If a woman had me wanting to be all that I could for her and to better myself for our future, then she was the woman for me. No woman had ever done that for me but Treasure.

Chapter Thirteen

GOOSE

I had some information on Crystal and how she put in for a legal name change in Miami, FL some months back. My private investigator located an address listed for a Sparkle Reynolds, which was the name on the name change application. I was happy as hell that she was alive, but that quickly faded when I realized she purposely faked her death and left me. When we married, I said it was until death do us part, so she has a rude awakening coming if she thought she could leave me and go live happily ever fucking while I been here hurting and going crazy. I took a few lines of that white girl to get my mind right for this drive to Florida. I was going to bring my wife home, and this time she wasn't leaving me unless it was death, and with how I felt, I was ready to end her ass and get me a new wife to take her place.

My mind was racing as I headed down the interstate. I knew our relationship was rocky but damn she really pulled a Lifetime movie move on my ass and got ghost faking her death for two years now. If this bitch was with another nigga, I was killing both of them and that way my grieving wouldn't have to be in vain. I'd move along now knowing that she really is dead. If she didn't want to be with me cool, but the only other choice was to be with your maker. I don't know what the hell she thought, but I was about to fix all this mess real soon. I was doing 90 all the way there with a vengeance.

Arriving in Florida, I decided to hit up a homie of mine to grab some of that bomb Florida weed and some percs. The women were every-thing out here, and they were walking by with everything on display on the strip. I had an ex from way back out this way that I was planning on hitting up. Rori was a dope ass chick, but she was too damn inde-pendent and never listened, so when she decided after high school to move to Miami, I let her go and damn do I regret that shit. I saw her Instagram, and baby girl was doing the damn thing out here. She had a badass house, car, and the whole nine, so I slid right in her DMs and said what was needed to secure me a meet up for tonight.

My next stop was by these condos Crystal/Sparkle or whatever the fuck she wanted to go by for now is cool because soon it a be dead bitch. I pulled up and was stuck admiring this beautiful park-like setting behind a huge metal gate. I watched for a few before I became bored and decided I would need more time to devise my plan on getting inside and to her door. I'd got my confirmation from Rori that I could meet her at the Ritz Carlton in an hour. I stopped off at the raggedy ass motel that I'd got for myself because I wasn't trying to spend my money on no lavish room when I was here on business.

I showered and threw on my Balenciaga fit dressed to impress and get a spot next to Rori for the time being. She liked all that fancy flashy shit, so I played my part and looked like new money. I popped my percs and was on my way to see Miss Rori.

Chapter Fourteen

TREASURE

W atching the beautiful blue waves as they crashed up on the beach laying on Honour's chest was everything to me. He handled me completely different than Shyne ever did, and I knew that was because I was not only dealing with a grown ass man but a real boss. We had just finished snorkeling and dirt bike racing with Sparkle and Pharaoh who seemed not to be able to keep their hands off each other hence the reason they went back to the room before our dinner later tonight at this authentic Dominican spot that Honour found for us. I was trying to keep my good girl image, but Honour was making it so hard not to take the D, and we haven't even made it exclusive yet.

Everything with Honour was flowing and moving fast to me, but life was short, and I was ready to live it. I didn't care that he was my ex's boss. That was Shyne's problem, not mine. Shyne left me looking stupid so many times and now the tables have turned and not on purpose, but I just have no fucks to give. One man's trash is another man's treasure is the saying, and in this case, I was now being valued by a real man. Honour made it so easy to fall head over heels for him, and not just because he was sexy and had a body of a Greek god. He was cool funny as hell and easy to be around. The talks we had were every-thing, and Honour was so intelligent. He talked about things with substance and not just the typical food, movies, and other bullshit. I mean we talked about those things too, but to be able to have an intellectual conversation was a completely different level from what I was used to.

We finally headed in to get dressed and ready for dinner at La Yola restaurant. I had decided to dress cute and sexy in a beach attire since we had a private dining tent set up on the beach with a personal outdoor staff and chef. I showered and did my makeup while Honour did the same in the guest bathroom, giving me the master suite. I wore a pink spandex one-piece bathing suit with a flowy pleated pink chiffon see-through skirt, and some crystal embellished strappy wedge heels. I pulled my bundles up into a ponytail and placed my diamond stud earrings in my ears. I had stopped wearing the jewelry that Shyne had given me over the years because I realized they were ways to keep and control me. I plan to send it all back to him when I return to Miami so that I can put the past behind me. Sparkle suggested I sell it all and keep the money and I think that was a great idea.

We had the perfect night at dinner, and now we all were heading to the hottest club on the resort. As we neared the club, I could hear Rihanna's "Work" blaring from the outdoor speakers. The line was down the beachfront, but Honour led the way skipping the line and entering through the VIP entrance. He never ceased to amaze me, and upon entering, we were escorted to a private section near the back. There were ladies dressed in Caribbean attire from the fancy headwear down to the bare feet adorned in foot jewels and ankle chains. They carried sparklers with the bottles of Dom, Ace of Spades, and Bellaire in each hand. We had two bottles each to ourselves amongst us four and the night was just beginning.

Honour pulled me close as I danced and twerked to Cardi B's "Bodak Yellow" all on him. We danced for damn near an hour straight before I finally took a seat. The Ace of Spades was catching up to me, and I couldn't stand without swaying from side to side. I was giggling my ass off at Sparkle because she was past her limit and was getting loose on the pole in our section. Pharaoh was enjoying the show and started throwing bands all over Sparkle, making it rain. I loved them together, and I was so happy for my friend. I took a few more sips of my drink before getting up and going to the other pole to show out a little for Honour.

I had taken many pole classes to stay fit, and now I was gone put what I learned to use. Migos "Motorsport" featuring Nicki Minaj and Cardi B came on, and I started to bounce my ass around watching Honour over my shoulder. He scooted up to the front of the lounge sofa he was seated on giving me his undivided attention. When I saw him adjust himself in his pants and bite his bottom lip, I knew I had him all in. I started making it clap, and he wasted no time throwing some bands at me and cheering me on to fuck it up. By the time the song was done, he had his hands all over me. We left the club on lit, and I knew tonight I'd be getting my share of some good baecation loving.

Chapter Fifteen

HONOUR

Treasure fucked my head up with the moves she was doing back at the club. Our walk down the beach back to our villa was taking too long. I was ready to tear her ass up right on the beach. Shit, who am I lying to, I was ready to sit her on my lap back at the club. I watched her round ass sway from side to side with a jiggle as she strutted along the beach like she was on a runway. Her round ass ate up the panty bottoms under her see-through skirt, and I had a clear view that had my shit rock hard. We made sure Pharaoh and Sparkle got into their villa safe and sound because they were more done of the liquor than we were. My nigga P was in love, and I knew it from the way he was with Sparkle. It was all about her and whatever she wanted. I couldn't even front though I wanted that with Treasure, and I was putting in the time and work to make that happen.

Sparkle was a good look for my boy. Maybe it'll slow his wild ass down because Pharaoh was headed nowhere fast with all the hoes he had chasing after him. Pharaoh be ready for whatever and that's why he's my right hand and my hitta that's trained to go, no questions asked. Nevertheless, we weren't getting one day younger, so it was time to build a family to share this wealth with from the empire we've built over the years. My mother was more than ready for me to have a family. My sister Honesty was attending Spelman, leaving my mother home with her two dogs alone, wanting to have some grandbabies. My mother raised us on her own for most of our lives with no help. My father was on and off that shit all my life, and when he called himself beating on my momma, she had him locked up, and we left Charlotte to head to Miami where her sister was for a better life. Mama never liked Miami though, so once I got the money, I moved her to Georgia where she really wanted to be.

Moving to Miami opened my eyes to what was out in these streets. I had a little hustle back in Charlotte, mostly weed and prescription pills. I came to Miami and only had my mom, sister, my Aunt Sylvia and my cousins Pharaoh, Cairo, and their baby sister Nile grew up with my sister Honesty. The girls were a year apart, so they were damn near raised as sisters. Our family was tight, and we made the best of things. I got put on early after I witnessed a robbery gone wrong as I delivered some weed to this cat name Vern who ran little Haiti. I saw these Mexican cats try to rob a worker of Vern's. They took off without all the work that he had because they man was hit in the process of the robbery by the nigga they were robbing. They killed who they were after and took off with a bag of money. I was duck off behind a garbage dumpster filming the whole thing on my Motorola Razr flip phone.

I took the work and video to Vern, who was ready to take my head off thinking I had something to do with it, but once I pointed out the Mexicans that he had an ongoing beef with, he let my ass live. The one condition and that was to prove myself by working for him and under him. The rest is history. After I eventually put in enough work, Vern passed that shit down to me when he went back to Haiti to retire. Here I was eight years, later at twenty-eight, running my own empire with my cousins Pharaoh and Cairo next to me. I wanted to wrap this shit up by the age of thirty and give it over to Cairo.

We were grooming Cairo to be next in line with his crew that he had with him, so I knew they would do just as good as we did. Cairo was only twenty-two, but he was wise beyond his age and level headed. Beyond the exterior, he was a ruthless ass nigga at heart, and he had a smart head on his shoulders. I knew he was destined to be a leader the way he carried himself out here. Here I am now ready to wrap this street shit up after I had a few close calls, but I'm still here, and I know when to walk away, and that's soon, real soon.

We finally reached our villa, and Treasure was eyeing me up and down as she sipped her Fiji water by the bar. I was ready, but I needed to know how prepared she was. I poured me a shot and then sparked up my blunt I had waiting from earlier. I took a few pulls and threw my shot back, ready to get down to business. I took a few more pulls and was just about to turn on the bar stool to see what Treasure was doing, but to my surprise, she was already up on me turning my seat to face her.

I damn near choked when I realized she was butt ass naked in front of me. Everything from her hot pink pedicured toes was perfect up to her flawless face that barely had makeup on it. She was on ten, and I loved this shit. Baby girl wasted no time undoing my belt and getting my shorts off. I helped her by standing up and letting her pull my pants down with my boxer briefs. I removed my polo and wife beater, and the only thing I wore was my Rolex and Cuban link chain. I watched as her hot pink manicured hands begun to rub and roam all over my abs until she reached my wood that was on brick just from her touch and presence.

She began to slow stroke alternating hands back and forth, and I knew I was gone off her because that shit felt so damn good, and she hadn't even used her mouth. She was like a damn masseuse, and the shit was feeling damn good. I never felt so relaxed and pleased all at the same time. I was about to pull her up, but she had other plans of her own. Without warning, she inched the head of my nine inches into her hot wet mouth, causing me to release a growl and moan out all at once.

Treasure began to take in more inches while still using her hands to stroke and jack my wood, and that was enough because I was about to be cumming down her throat if she kept going. I pulled back to stop her, and she let my wood pop out her mouth sexily. I reached down, pulling her up into my arms where we began to kiss sloppily as my hands roamed her body.

I needed to taste her and see if she was as sweet as I imagined, and with all the tropical fruits we'd been eating here, I know she had sweet nectar by now. I turned her, so she was now against the bar stool. I turned her around, bent her over, and spread her ass cheeks so that her pussy was no longer hiding but now playing peek-a-boo. I ran my tongue up her folds, causing her to shudder and moan out in pleasure. I used my tongue to separate her lips as I invaded her honey pot that immediately dripped like a leaking faucet as I pushed my tongue further in. I received a gush of the sweetest nectar of pussy juice I ever had. It was all over. Treasure was mine, and I was for damn sure hers from this moment I was in love with the smell the taste the sight and feel of her.

I was slurping and lapping her up like this was my last meal and the moans she released let me know a nigga was doing his job. All her juices were coating my beard, and I welcomed that with no worries. As her man, it was my job to please her. I had a hunger so deep for her that it surprised me because it's been a minute since I wanted to eat some pussy, let alone be enjoying it. I felt her pussy muscles contracting on my tongue, and I knew she was about to cum. I started to suck on her swollen clit and inserted two fingers stroking her g-spot, and that took her over the edge. She began to squirt and shake calling out to me and anyone in the distance on the beach that could hear her.

I let her recover as I strapped up with a condom ready for the main attraction. I helped her to stand up straight, but I realized she had them orgasm legs that wouldn't let her stand up yet. I decided to take control of this show and get shit cracking. I picked her up, allowing her to wrap her arms around my neck and legs around my back, locking them together. I thought she was out for the count, but she started to twerk her ass around on my pole, causing me to grip her ass cheeks that sat perfectly in the palm of my hands.

Treasure began to suck on my neck, and I couldn't wait until we reached the room. I slid her down on my pole slowly, and her eyes got big as we locked in a stare down as I took my time guiding her down all nine inches. Once fully in her tight tunnel, I was on cloud nine.

She could ask me to give her all my money, shit a nigga will give her his last name, all the money, and a lung if she wanted it, as long as this little slice of heaven was always mine. I never pulled out as I walked us to the room. I slid up into the bed with Treasure on top of me now not once slipping out. I laid back with my hands behind my head and let her do her thang.

The sound of the wind and the water hitting the beach was soothing as the moonlight shined through the wide open patio doors. Treasure wasted no time planting her feet on each side of my legs in a squat position as she began to bounce up and down in my lap. I enjoyed the show as I massaged and squeezed her nipples as she rode my shit like a pro.

I wasn't gone be able to hold out much longer with how tight and wet she was, so I flipped her onto all fours and stood up on the side of the bed pulling her to the edge. I gave her a few slow deep strokes before I started to pound her out, ready to bust this nut. Treasure was keeping up throwing her ass back making it clap for me.

"You know this pussy mine, now, right?" I asked and then slapped her on the ass, waiting for an answer.

"Yessss, Honour! It's yours, baby!" she screamed out in ecstasy as I gave her deeper slow strokes, nearing my peak.

"Cum for me, Treasure. Yeah sexy, throw that ass back at me," I was coaching her to an orgasm. I felt her muscles contract and then clamp down, so I knew she was about to let loose.

"Ooooh, daddy, I'm cumming!" I couldn't even respond as we both let go of the biggest nuts that I had in a long ass time.

I took a minute to recover and admire her sexy ass sprawled out over the bed. I scooped her up so that we could shower and lay down in a dry bed. After showering, we laid in the guest room instead of the master since the covers were drenched from Treasure. I made sure to leave a note for housekeeping not to disturb us in the guest room but to handle the rest of the villa. Treasure was knocked out beside me still butt naked and glowing in the night light. I felt like a lucky ass man to have a beautiful, good woman who had dreams and didn't care about the money I made, but instead, took the time to get to know the real me.

I knew before we got to serious, I'd have to take her to Atlanta to meet my mama and Honesty because I needed their approval to add another important lady to my life outside of them. I had a feeling they would all get along just fine.

I checked a few of my messages and missed calls as Treasure snored lightly beside me. One message stood out to me, and I knew it was about to be some shit when we got back to Miami. Cairo said Shyne was around talking big shit about how I left him hanging in the streets, and he was about to take over. However, the part that had me hot was the money he was offering for info on Treasure. I would wait until our trip was over to see where her head was at with that situation and how she wanted to handle it.

My way of handling Shyne would erase him entirely from being an issue for me altogether. They had history, and I never wanted to hurt Treasure, but I knew how Shyne was, and he was going to be a problem, especially once he found out that I had Treasure with me, and she was never coming back to him.

I was far from cocky, but I was confident. Shit was different with Treasure, and I knew she was exactly where I wanted to be. The way we vibe and connect was a force to be reckoned with. I wasn't letting anyone come in between what we were building, and if Shyne tried, I'd have to take care of him. In all honesty, he had it coming from the fuck shit he had already done, but if he tried anything with Treasure now that she was mine, I wasn't letting anything slide.

Chapter Sixteen

SHYNE

It had been damn near a month since I had seen or heard from Treasure. I left so many voicemails that her shit was now full and couldn't receive anymore. I was starting to feel sick at the thought she ran off with another nigga. I decided to make an Instagram page so that I could follow her and see what she was up to. I made a fake make-up page with a bunch of different makeup looks and styles so that she wouldn't suspect that it was me.

To my surprise, her page was public. I noticed that she had a lot of new posts up and in the last one she is laid on the beach looking sexy as hell with a two-piece bikini that had her body on full display. She already had thousands of likes, and I was about to leave the page until I saw a post from two days ago of her at a club looking good as hell as if she was having the time of her life.

The shit that threw me though was the nigga she was with. I couldn't see his face, but his hands were all over her body as she twerked and posed for the camera. His face was hidden from the picture, and that shit had me pissed because I needed to get at whoever had my baby disappearing on me. I looked a little further down in her posts, and she had a picture with her and Sparkle on jet skis. So, she was on vacation not caring at all that I was out here looking for her thinking her ass was snatched up possibly behind my shit. If this bitch thought that she could leave me, she was crazy as hell. I owned Treasure, and I was gone show her ass not to fuck with me.

I needed to catch up with Rori. She had been avoiding and dodging me this whole week. I first had to stop by this older cat Yunil's house to grab up this work since Honour cut me off. I needed some work, so I had to find the next best thing, and although Yunil's shit wasn't grade A, I could still make some shit happen with his product. I slid through his spot first before popping up to Rori's house. Her car was there but a black old school Chevy was also in her driveway. If this bitch had a nigga up in here, I was gone fuck her and that nigga up.

I rang the bell and waited for a few minutes, but I had no answer. I rang again pushing the bell a few more times growing irritated. I was about to start banging on the door, but Rori swung the door open looking high as hell, but sexy as fuck in her bra panties and sheer robe. I walked right in, and she smacked her teeth at me, slamming the door closed. I turned around and charged her up against the wall. I squeezed her throat just enough to scare her, so she knew not to play with me, but not enough that she couldn't breathe.

Her eyes got wide as she tried to squirm, and my grip tightened. I let her go and pushed her towards the stairs so that we could go upstairs, but I was stopped in my tracks by some big nigga coming out the bathroom and down the hallway humming and shit.

I looked from Rori to him, and him to Rori, and he just threw me a head nod and kept going to the kitchen like he was at home around this bitch. I turned to Rori, who backed away in fear of seeing my fist balled up beside me. I was grilling her ass waiting for an explanation because title or not, she knew she belonged to me and only me, and I'd kill her and this nigga if she were on any bullshit with me. I snatched Rori up and pushed her up the stairs, and once we reached her room, I slammed her door closed and locked it.

"Who the fuck is that big ass nigga, Rori?" I spoke through clenched teeth right in her face. I was so pissed that I wanted to smack fire from her ass.

"That's Goose, a nigga I know from back home in Savannah. He reached out on Facebook looking to get put on to some work. I got him lined up with Tech and his crew out in LA. That's where he will be going after he finds his ex-wife. You can help him and make some good money in the process. His ex-wife is Crystal, but she goes by Sparkle now," Rori spoke with a smirk on her face. She knew all about my hatred towards Sparkle because I felt she was in Treasure ear to leave me.

The info that Rori gave to me had my interest piqued, so I agreed to discuss plans with her and this Goose nigga. I didn't care for this nigga one bit, so I was keeping my eye on him. I wasn't feeling how comfortable he was up in Rori's house dressed in just a wife beater and sweats and some Nike slides like he was right at home. He drank the rest of the Minute Maid fruit punch from the carton and sat at the table like he was the HNIC. The man hadn't been here more than a few days and was chilling as if he was right at home, and Rori's silly as went right along with whatever he said like a retard.

We were all seated at Rori's dining room table ready to discuss the plan and come to find out we were now up against way bigger problems. We confirmed on Instagram that Sparkle was dating Pharaoh, Honour's right hand man and cousin, which got me to thinking that Treasure was probably talking to Cairo who was Pharaoh's brother. This bitch was probably fucking with this nigga the whole time playing me. I have been paying the bills regardless if I was out doing me she was supposed to stick to the script and sit her ass down, but I had a trick up my sleeve for her ass.

I knew Honour had to know something, so I was heading to see him once we were done ironing out the details of our plan. I let them do most of the talking so I could feel out this nigga Goose. He seemed like a clown to me, fake tough guy who thought he pumped fear in someone's heart. If Sparkle was once the woman that ran out on him, then I wonder why. He obviously wasn't shit if she dipped out and fake her death. He probably was a weak man beating her down. I mean every now and again you got give them some act right, but to beat on your woman you were a bitch in my opinion.

I watched Rori as she laughed and giggled at this nigga's weak jokes. She probably was ready to fuck with his hoe ass. I was gone keep a real close eye on her ass too because she was starting to move real funny, and I see it's because of her company. We were about to come up in a big way and take out all the pawns in our way, or so we thought.

Chapter Seventeen

TREASURE

We were heading to the airport finally on our way home from our weeklong vacation. I sat in the back of the limo with a massive hangover with my shades over my eyes while resting my throbbing head back on the seat. I was having flashbacks of the amazing sex that Honour woke me up to this morning. I was having those pulsating heart throbs in my kitty reminding me of the nice pounding I had this morning just hours prior. I had only ever been with my first and Shyne, so I always thought Shyne was the best dick I ever had, but Honour came and changed my mind on that. I can't ever remember being sexed so good, and my new obsession was Honour and all things him.

You usually take your time and get to know each other better, but I threw all the caution to the wind and just went with what I felt, and I was feeling happier than I ever had. Everything with Honour was smooth, and nothing felt forced or fake. We connected and built in a short time what Shyne and I never had. Honour made me feel like I mattered and made me feel like my goals were a priority to him. The first line of business when we returned was getting my things from the condo. I was not looking forward to that task because I had a feeling that I'd have to see Shyne in order to get my things. I was tempted to take Honour's offer of a shopping spree and get all new items, but I had already been spoiled enough by him, plus some of my things were irreplaceable and held sentimental value.

We made it home safe and sound. I decided to hold off on going to get my things until the morning when Sparkle could accompany me. We decided while the guys were out handling business, we could grab up my things and avoid any drama. I also planned to look for an apartment tomorrow as well. Honour insisted on me staying with him even if I took the guest room as my own. He just wanted me under the same roof with him. I thought it was cute how Honour didn't want me away from him. He even talked about going to school with me. Honour was very tech savvy, and I told him he should take up Computer Information at the school. He said he might start with a few classes just to see since he hadn't been to school in quite some time.

I loved the fact that he had other goals in life outside of the streets. I knew exactly what Honour did and who he was, but he had a good head on his shoulders and wasn't irresponsible with his money or how he handled his business. Shyne should have been paying attention and taking notes, but oh well, his problem. I still hadn't returned any of his voicemails and the last one he threatened to become physical the minute he found me. I usually brush off the things he says, but he sounded serious this time. I hadn't told Honour because I didn't want to bring him any stress or drama behind my ex. I told Treasure, and she promised not to tell Pharaoh or Honour but signed us up for self-defense lessons and got us some tasers. My next step was getting my pistol permit because if I had to, I'd shoot Shyne if he thought that he could he hurt me.

Honour had left me alone in his huge home, and I decided to cook and chill until he came back. I wasn't a five-star chef, but I could do a few things. I decided on fried chicken, mashed potatoes, and a salad. I was startled by the sound of the doorbell as I removed the last batch of chicken from the deep fryer. I didn't know if I should open his door but decided to at least check the camera in the hall where the alarm system was. I looked at the camera and was immediately frozen in place staring at Shyne on the camera. He was dressed in all black with a hood halfway over his head.

I decided to call Honour and let him know what was going on. I was dialing the number when the bell rang again startling me yet again. My hands were shaking, and my heart was racing a mile a minute.

The phone rang over to voicemail, and I told Honour it was important that he call me right away. I then called up Treasure, and she didn't answer either. I was having a full-on panic attack, and the bell rang one last time. I went back to the monitor, and Shyne was getting in his car to leave. I pray he leaves and doesn't come back. I went to the kitchen to grab a drink, and my phone started to ring. I picked up on the first ring and told Honour that Shyne had just left, but I didn't open the door. He told me to make sure the locks were on, and the alarm was set and to sit tight. He was on his way.

Sparkle called back as well, and I filled her in on the info. She told me she would be on her way, but I stopped her letting her know Honour was heading home. I showered and lounged in the living room watching *Good Girls* on Netflix. I had just got up to get a drink from the bar when Honour finally walked in from the back where the garage was. He rushed over to me, checking me like I was hurt, and I just laughed at him before kissing his lips.

"You sure you good? You didn't open up the door for him, right?" he asked while pulling me down into his lap on the recliner.

"Yes, baby, I'm sure I'm ok, and no, I never opened the door. Why would he come here?" I asked, sipping on the glass of wine I had poured.

"He's probably pissed he can't make no moves in my city anymore period, not just off my team. He can't get put on at all with anybody, so I assume that is why. Who knows we have been flooding Instagram and Facebook with or pictures, so I'm sure people are talking. That's how it goes. The streets talk, and he probably came looking for you. Are you having a change of mind about us?" he asked, staring intensely into my eyes.

"No, Honour, not at all. I have never been as happy as I am now with anyone else. You are where I want to be," I said truthfully, never breaking our intense stare.

"Good because I meant what I said when I said you were mine once I blessed you with this dope dick." He laughed before kissing my neck.

I was laughing, but that soon turned to moans of pleasure from the way he was kissing on me. We started to kiss passionately and undress each other, but the ringing of Honour's phone interrupted us. He lifted me off him so that he could stand up to get the phone out his back pocket. He answered the phone and let out a few displeased sighs before hanging the phone up.

"I got to run out really quick for a last-minute emergency meeting. Lock up, and I'll be back as soon as I can," he said, kissing my forehead and then my lips.

"Ok, be careful, Honour. I'll be right here when you get back," I assured him. He was out the door, and I set the code and went to finish watching my show.

I don't remember what time I fell asleep, but waking up in Honour's arms as he slept was the best thing ever. I slowly removed myself from his embrace so that I could go to the bathroom. I had one too many glasses of wine, and I was paying for it with these frequent bathroom trips. I went to the bathroom and then returned ready to climb right back in bed to snuggle with Honour, but Cola had other plans. Cola sat by the patio doors off Honour's room waiting to go out. I guess she needed to relieve her bladder just as I had done. I let her out the door and sat in one of the patio chairs while she handled her business. The backyard was so peaceful and huge. It looked like I was in a park and not the back of a house.

I heard noises off to the side, so I grabbed Cola up and ran inside to wake Honour up. It sounded like two guys talking and messing with the gate to the backyard. The back of Honour's house faced a highway, so noise was expected, but not the sound of someone trying to pry open a gate. I shook Honour awake, and he looked up at me, smiling widely still half sleep. This man was so damn fine that I almost forgot about what the hell I needed to tell him from just one look in his face.

"Honour, baby, wake up. Some men are messing with the back gate," I said in a higher pitched voice than usual.

"Go in the guest room and lock the door!" he shouted as he jumped up, grabbing his gun from the nightstand and rushing to the hallway.

I could hear the emergency alarm system being activated. I peeked out the blinds and could see the alarm lights flashing and an automated voice advising intruders to get back. I heard shots ring out, and I screamed, dropping to the floor. I was scared as hell and didn't know what the hell was going on. The Shot fire ceased, and the alarm was disarmed. I heard Honour calling for me, and I was still frozen in fear, unable to move. The door handle jiggled as Honour tried to get inside. I jumped up hands shaking, palms sweating and raced over to the door. I unlocked the door, and he pulled me in and hugged me tightly. I hadn't realized I had tears until he wiped them away.

"Is everything ok? What were all the damn shots I heard?" I asked frantically.

"Yes, beautiful, everything is ok. That is the monthly testing of my system, and it helps my senses to be in high gear if anything was to ever happen. I run this drill once a month in a different area of the house each time to train for moments just like this. God forbid, but in my line of work, I have to stay ten steps ahead of all my enemies known and unknown," he stated calmly, grabbing my hand to lead me out the room, but I snatched away because I was pissed off that I was put into a damn test with no warning.

"Are you fucking kidding me, Honour? Why wouldn't you tell me something like this? I pissed in my damn pants out of fear. I thought I was about to die, and you were running a drill and didn't think to put me up on game!"

I stormed past him to the bathroom so that I could get my pissy ass in the shower. Honour pulled me back and turned me to face him. I was beyond pissed and his sexy smirk wasn't gone change that.

"I have to prepare you, and if I tell you, then you wouldn't have acted quickly and alerted me as you should have. I wasn't even sleep for real, but I had to get you ready. This not that life you lived with Shyne. I got real boss nigga problems, and at any given moment that shit can pop off just as the drill did. So, I apologize you were put in a position to feel embarrassed, but with me baby, you never have to be embarrassed. Trust, you will thank me later for this. Now let's go shower, and I'm a get my shooter over here to give you some gun lessons," he said, kissing me softly and pulling me towards the bathroom.

Chapter Eighteen

PHARAOH

I knew Honour took safety and staying ahead of all enemies known and unknown seriously, so I wasn't surprised when he told me about running a drill on Treasure last night. It was funny as hell though when he told me shorty pissed on herself. Sparkle cursed me and Honour out bad for clowning on her girl. Messing around with Honour, Sparkle had dipped off on my ass with Treasure to have a girl's day. I decided to make my rounds and check on my brother, Cairo. Cairo was laid back and chill, but a straight savage at heart. He didn't care about anything but the money, so I knew he was out getting to it. My brother was getting older, and I feel like he needs to find him a good woman, but he'd rather take down a thot and send her on her way. Shit, I don't blame him truthfully, I used to be the same dam way, but Sparkle changed my whole mindset.

Cairo handled the logistics of the product and the distribution among the workers. Cairo had a foolproof plan that involved a mortuary and empty John Doe's. Cairo ran the mortuary as if he was about to cremate all the John Doe's but instead, he had staff that would empty them, fill it with product or cash, and transport the bodies across the country to our clients. We had mortuary locations all over to receive shipments and complete the transactions. Cairo ran this part of the operation with ease, so we stepped back and let him do his thing. He went through school, obtaining a Mortuary Science degree and becoming an Undertaker. He didn't provide funeral services, but on paper and in the books that's exactly how things appeared, making our life less stressed about moving all the weight we did.

I did all that I needed to within an hour tops and was on my way to see my brother. I never spent too much time at the funeral home because the shit gave me the creeps. I never understood how he just worked all day in that damn place and acted as if it was no big deal. I pulled up and parked in the reserved spaces along the front of the building. It was a beautiful day out, and I wanted to take Sparkle to the pier and get ice cream and our picture painted. She had asked me a few weeks ago, and it slipped my mind with everything we had going plus taking our vacation. I entered the employee entrance with my badge and headed straight to the basement.

As I walked down the steps, I could hear the classical music playing, and all I could do was shake my head and laugh. This is the exact reason why this nigga was single. No female was putting up with the weirdo shit he does, and they all will probably run once they realized how obsessed he was with these dead bodies. My brother was something special, and I knew since we were kids. He enjoyed science and dissecting shit, so this only makes sense that he would enjoy stuffing these dead bodies and cutting them open to retrieve packages. I turned the corner into his workroom and almost threw up. Just as I was coming in, he was pulling organs out of a man's body and tossing them in a large bin.

I had to close my eyes and count to ten before proceeding. I could kill a motherfucker and then have someone dispose of a body, but this shit was way out my league and made me sick to my stomach. I walked over to the back area where the rows of pills and money were stacked high up the wall. It had to be over a half a million in here, not to mention over a million in product. This operation was taking on a life of its own outside of the typical weed, coke, and meth we pushed. Life was good compared to where we started. It was days we ain't eat, and times we had nowhere to sleep, but once mama got approved for disability, things got a little better.

"You counted this yet?" I asked, picking up a few stacks of money.

"Yea, it's all there just waiting for the next few bodies from the hospitals to arrive so that we can get the product shipped, and then the money will be deposited over time into our accounts so that we don't raise any suspicions. I got this, big bro," he replied, smiling and turning the music back up.

"I just came to check you out. I'ma bring Sparkle to Sunday dinner this weekend to meet mama," I stated before walking to the table and taking a peek inside one of the bodies he was working on.

"Dammmm, you feeling her like that? Man, now mama's gone be on me about settling down all because of you and your sucka for love ass," he retorted sounding annoyed but laughing.

"You should find you someone just as crazy as you to settle down with, man. You gone get all our parts of the business, so sooner or later you gone need a queen at home holding you down," I said before making my way out the door.

"I'll hit you later, bro. I might slide out with y'all tonight. I need a break from all the dead shit." He laughed at his own joke and caused me to laugh too. I continued out and went straight to see my lady.

Chapter Nineteen

HONOUR

I t took Treasure damn near twenty-four hours to talk to me after the whole home drill situation. I still laughed hard as hell every time I thought about it. My baby was scared as hell, and then pissed off as soon as I told her what was up. I had to get her trained to go as quickly as possible because shit could change up at any moment, and with Shyne still out searching for her, I needed her to be able to protect and defend herself. Last night we all went to the club and had a good time, and the ladies got to finally meet Cairo. After a few drinks, Treasure came around and was all over me. We didn't even make it out of the lot of the club when everyone else left because she wanted to ride me right there, and I didn't stop her. I was a squirrel in her world just trying to get a nut, literally it was whatever she wanted.

Today we were all driving down to Atlanta to surprise my mama with a visit so that she and Honesty could meet Treasure. I hadn't been to see them in a few months, so this trip was long overdue. I missed my favorite girls, but they were safer in Georgia and away from all my shit in Miami. We tried to work on Auntie Sylvia, but she didn't budge. She was born and raised in Florida and refused to leave. Honesty and Nile would be starting college in the fall, and with Nile heading down to Atlanta with Honesty and mama, I think Auntie Sylvia will move too. My family being away from any enemies known and unknown gives me peace of mind.

I was prepared for the attitude from Honesty since I wouldn't let her come to school in Miami, but she knows I will gladly pay for her to attend any school in Georgia, and with the help that Pharaoh and Cairo offered to help pay for an off-campus apartment for her and Nile, they should be straight. From my experience, Miami was no place for them, and at the age they were, they were liable to be sucked in and spit right back out. My baby sister was my heart and I had to protect her at all cost, by any means necessary. My mama was too damn lenient with Honesty, and that irked my nerves because Honesty knew how to finesse my mama into letting her do some bullshit that she knew she had no business doing, especially the shit I'd never approve of. Last time I came here, I went off and cut off her allowance for a month because she went and got her belly button pierced, and she wasn't even eighteen at that time.

Honesty stayed testing my gangster, but I never could stay too mad at her for long. I just wanted the best for her and with our pops never consistently around, I tried to be a father figure to her and set a good example. I wanted my baby sister to marry a nigga better than me, not like me. She needed to find a doctor, lawyer, or business professional. She needed to be successful and then a wholesome housewife, but if she did things the way she preferred, she'd be on a pole or lined up for a twerk contest trying to get "Flewed Out". I hated that periodt shit that the City Girls was screaming. These ratchets had taken over mainstream music and social media with bald headed hoe activities. They glorified taking niggas money to up they own bag, and I refused to see Honesty out here like that now, period that shit.

The ride was about nine and a half hours, so we packed bags to stay for the weekend. I had only let one person meet my mama before, and that was Tuesday. My mama never cared for her and had met her once and told me to leave her alone and never bring her around again. I wasn't worried about Treasure though. I was confident mama would love her and give her approval. I also had a few business associates in Atlanta that I needed to meet up with and discuss a few deals for expansion of my business, but I also had plans to be a silent investor in a new strip club.

I met Styles years ago on a few trips to Buffalo I had to make when I first got started. He was a few years younger than I was but was ready to make moves. I told him I'd add him to the team once his Uncle Stoney told me I was a go. Things were looking good until he had to go do a bid. I worked closely with his uncle and cousin Sincere, and when he was released, he told me he wasn't going to the streets now that he had to be here for his family. When Styles' cousin Sincere died, he put a hold on the strip club due to funding and other things, so I offered to be a silent partner/investor. I had the utmost respect for Styles and the move he was making, so this was only right.

Pulling into my mama's driveway, I shut the car off and sat in silence for a few. I'd done the whole drive here with Pharaoh following behind me with his mama, Sparkle, and sister in the car with him. I needed just to sit and relax after that drive. I hadn't seen Pharaoh pull in yet, so I figured he was a few minutes behind. I'd wait for him and the ladies so that we all could surprise mama and Honesty.

I was growing a little impatient after fifteen minutes of waiting on Pharaoh and them to come, so I texted him to see where they were. Pharaoh let me know his mama wanted to stop at Publix and get groceries to cook breakfast for everyone. He said they should be here in about twenty minutes, so I let Treasure sleep and laid my seat back to get a quick nap in.

I tried to sleep but couldn't. After ten minutes of just sitting there, I decided to get out and get the luggage out and on the porch. Just as I was closing the trunk, I heard noises off to the side of my mama's house. It was five in the morning, and I knew my mama was still sleeping. She has woken up at seven a.m every day for as long as I can remember. I pulled my gun from my hip and made my way slowly to the side. I peeked around the corner and saw Honesty with some nigga in the backyard laid up on a hammock with his hands all over her. I lost all sense and charged towards them. Honesty looked like a deer caught in headlights when I snatched her up, causing homeboy to flip off the hammock and hit the grass. He jumped up quick looking like he was ready to throw hands.

"Honour, what is wrong with you?" Honesty yelled, stomping her feet like the little girl she was.

"What's wrong with me? What the hell is wrong with you having this nigga up in mama house this early? Honesty, you're eighteen, not twenty-eight!" I roared at her peering down into her innocent looking face.

"Well, eighteen is grown to me, especially when I go away to school. You don't run my life, Honour. I love you big bro, but you have to let me live. Come on, Shaw. I'll walk you out to your car," she replied, walking out, leaving me in the yard pissed off.

"Nah let me holla at him first. Since you're so grown, the least you can do is introduce him to me," I stated, stopping them in their tracks.

Honesty and the guy made their way back over and I looked him up and down observing him closely. He appeared to be about her age, so I gave them a pass on that and relaxed a little bit. She introduced him as her friend Shaw. She stated he was from California and was in Georgia visiting with family before heading back out to Cali the next day. He seemed like an ok guy, but I noticed the massive amount of blue he wore, so it didn't take a rocket scientist to figure out what set he claimed. He was a Crip for sho. He was laid back and chill. He said he's in the studio sometimes, and he wanted to tattoo and have his own shop, so I pumped my big bro brakes on them and let them rock out. I had more to discuss with Honesty about this school situation, but I'd save that for later.

I heard the music bumping as I walked back to the front, just as I came from the backyard Pharaoh was pulling into the driveway.

I helped him bring all the bags on the porch and rang the bell for mama to let us in. About five minutes later, I heard the alarm being disarmed, and the door came open. My mother was in her robe and headscarf, but still was the most beautiful woman I had ever seen. Her face and eyes lit up, and a huge smile crept on her face as she pulled me in for a hug. Mama squeezed me so tight, but it felt good to have her love on me. Mama was my queen for real.

"You bet not ever stay away that long again, boy," she chastised me with a pointed finger.

"Not at all, mama, I'm sorry. I meant to visit sooner, but I've been busy. I call you every day though," I replied, laughing at her scowl and mean mug.

"That ain't the same. Now, get out my way so that I can see the rest of my family," she said, pushing me to the side.

They all hugged and embraced, and Treasure stood off to the side of the car with Sparkle. I signaled both of them to come on up to the door. They took their time walking slowly as hell to the stairs.

"Ma, I want you to meet my lady Treasure and her best friend, Sparkle," I said as they came up on the porch.

"That fine one there belongs to me, Auntie. That's my baby!" Pharaoh yelled out from inside the house, causing us all to laugh.

We all got acquainted and talked while mama and Auntie Sylvia cooked the food. Nile and Honesty took off to her room after they met the girls. I questioned mama about this Shaw boy, and she said that he and Honesty have been talking for a little while now and she approves, and that's all that matters. That's what she thinks, but I had already texted my peoples out in Cali to do a thorough check on this cat because if he was gone be around my sister, I needed to know all there is to know about him and who he affiliated with. Apparently, I had let my absence create this issue because Honesty had dropped the bomb on me that she and Nile would be going to college in California and not to Spelman. I wasn't feeling that at all, and I would be checking further into that.

Chapter Twenty

SPARKLE

I had finally found the time to go over to my abandoned apartment as I call it. After the weekend with Pharaoh and Honour's family, he had me at his house all week holding me hostage, but I loved every minute of it. Today he had some things to handle with his brother Cairo, so I decided to head over to my apartment and at least see it since I'd been away for so long. If Pharaoh had it his way, I'd be moving in with him because he always wanted me in the house to greet him when he came home. He has stayed over a few times at my apartment, but the neighbors be cooking Indian food, and he hates the smell.

I parked in my space and climbed out, checking my surroundings as I always do. I had become way more relaxed than when I first got here, but for some reason, the last few days, I have felt as if I'm being watched or followed. I spoke to the doorman and the front desk clerk before checking my mailbox. Things were piled up high in my box almost unable to fit. I skimmed through some magazines and fliers as I rode the elevator up to my floor. I turned the corner and approached my door where an overflow of roses sat. Some looked old like they were delivered more than a week ago. I picked them up and searched high and low for a card, but there wasn't one. I opened the door taking all ten bouquets inside with me and stepped on a card that appeared to have been slid up under my door. I tossed the old roses and placed the newer ones in a vase. I ripped the card open, and it was a pretty all red card with a gold heart on the front.

I flipped it open and damned near lost my mind. A picture from me and Goose's shotgun wedding was glued to the inside. And the words *forever my love* was written in Goose's handwriting. I felt faint and started to panic all at once. How did he find me, and where is he now? The questions were running rampant through my mind as I raced to the back and grabbed my gun. I emptied my safe and packed my luggage. Everything else could stay. I had to get the hell out of this apartment and for good. I flew out of the house and raced back to Pharaoh's place. He still hadn't arrived, and I checked my surroundings to make sure that I wasn't followed. I paced back and forth, contemplating on if I should tell Pharaoh or not. I had never divulged my true identity or past to anyone. He knew nothing about my life prior other than the fact I had an ex who hurt me physically mentally and emotionally.

Crystal died a long time ago, and the woman I was as Sparkle was who I would be for the rest of my life. Changing my name and identity allowed me to start over and live the life I deserved and wanted. I didn't have to take care of a mother who was sick and dying and leaving me to fend for myself at eighteen. I was left with some money, but not much, and most of it Goose took from me. The money I hid totaled $200,000, and I was living off that now. I had plans here and with Pharaoh for our future, and I would do whatever it takes to make that happen. I knew the time would come that I would have to kill Goose or be killed, and I wanted to live, so I had to figure out a way to get rid of him for good.

For now, I'd stay with Pharaoh and figure out how to get rid of Goose. Hopefully, he has left Miami since he didn't see me or locate me, or so I hope. I hated this feeling of paranoia and not knowing what to expect. I felt so out of control of my life, and I didn't want to go back to living locked in a house out of fear that Goose would get me. I needed to take some more shooting lessons and self-defense classes so that I could protect myself at all cost. I refused to go down without a fight. Goose controlled my life long enough, and the freedom, happiness, and peace I have now meant everything to me. It's like the first hot summer day after a brutal winter and rainy spring. You want to relish in that moment and enjoy it.

For years, I dealt with abuse, both verbally and physically, at the hands of the husband who claimed to love me. I had no way to get out of the situation other than to do something drastic, and I had thought I had made the perfect plan and escape. The part I didn't do was haunting me now as I tried to live my new life. I had initially planned to kill Goose, but I couldn't bring myself to harm him even after all he had done to me. That was a detrimental decision that I'd made, and I wish I could go back and poison his meal that day I left for work, but no soft ass Crystal just had to have a heart of gold even for a low-down bastard like Goose. Goose had mental issues that he should have been on meds for, but he opted to self-medicate with coke, lean, weed, and any other pills.

I texted Pharaoh's phone telling him I had a surprise for him. I unpacked my luggage and placed my things in the closet he designated for me. I placed all my perfumes, lotions, and candles on the shelves in the walk-in closet, lined my shoes up, and I put my house shoes at the foot of the bed. I felt at home despite my paranoia and uneasiness about Goose. I pondered on the decision to tell Pharaoh tonight about Goose and my real name. I felt like we were connected and becoming one, yet he had no clue who I truly was. Sparkle and Crystal were apart of who I truly was, but Crystal had been the past and the weak side of me. Sparkle was so full of life and happiness that was the woman Crystal was supposed to be before life beat her down.

Pharaoh hit me back and said he was wrapping a few things up and he would be home shortly, so I decided to take a relaxing bubble bath and zone out to my Summer Walker playlist. I had candles lit, and a glass of wine poured and ready as I climbed inside the huge whirlpool Jacuzzi tub. The jets and bubbles instantly relaxed me. I let the words of "Girls Need Love" play and soothe my stresses away. I slowly felt my anxiety and paranoia subsiding, but in the pit of my stomach, I had a feeling something was going to happen and shake my peaceful world up into a frenzy.

Chapter Twenty-One

PHARAOH

Two Months Later

I was sweating bullets as I got ready for tonight's festivities. I had found the perfect ring for my perfect girl. Sparkle was everything a nigga needed, and more than I could want. She had a rough past that she'd yet to fully explain or elaborate on to me in full detail, but I loved her and would be patient and wait for her to tell me when she was ready. My mama, siblings, and the rest of my family, especially Honour, all loved her too and agreed she was right for me. My mother had started to call Sparkle more than she called me, and Nile had been hanging out with Sparkle, getting some sisterly bonding time in. They talked all the time and always went on shopping sprees with my black card, of course. I was happy to see all the ladies in my life get along, so it was only right I made things official and gave Sparkle my last name. Nile had helped me pick out the engagement ring and plan the engagement. Nile suggested that I propose on Sparkle's birthday. That way everyone was in attendance and Sparkle would never see it coming keeping it a surprise.

Her birthday fell on a Saturday, and that made it perfect for throwing a big birthday bash with a surprise engagement. The party was being held on the pier where we first met on the yacht. All these details were outside the norm for me and felt cheesy as hell, but for Sparkle, I'd do it a thousand times to prove my love and make her happy the way she made me. I couldn't front though a nigga was scared as hell of her possibly rejecting my proposal in front of everyone. I shared my nervous thoughts with Nile and Cairo, and they both were confident that she'd say yes.

I hired a fly ass event planner that planned events all over the country and outside the U.S. for top clients and celebrities. Prophecy came highly recommended with a high ass price tag too, especially for such a short notice event, but thanks to Honour and his business with the infamous and mysterious Phor, he put in a good word, and she accepted. The rumor was that Prophecy was Phor's secret child or some type of family, and that's how she got on as a celebrity event planner, but the answer would never be known because she refused to speak on Phor. I also had a recommendation from my realtor Seven while looking for properties to invest in Sparkle's dream.

One night while we laid up and watched shows on TV, Sparkle told me she had been working from home through Amazon just to save money and have income coming in until she could get a home. However, what blew my mind was when she said she wanted the home to be a safe house for women their children after being in a toxic environment or experiencing a huge loss like domestic violence or homelessness due to house fires, eviction, etc. She just wanted a place to help. So many people who were on the same path and felt they had no way to escape.

I decided that say I would do whatever to help make her dream happen, so when my realtor found some great locations, I jumped on them. I narrowed it down to three homes that I would show her next week as her last birthday surprise. I wanted to not only invest in her dreams, but I wanted to be there to experience every goal and milestone with her, and that's when I knew a player like myself had falling in love. Cupid hit my ass hard as hell with that arrow.

I had many talks about all my plans with my mama and Honour, and they had given me countless blessings to go with it. So, here we are. The day has come, and I was ready to ask the woman of my dreams to be my wife. It was going to be an epic night for Miami with the biggest party and biggest surprise they had ever seen. I had lined up some dope local artist for live entertainment, and I had fireworks for the proposal with a blimp with the words *will you marry me* across it all lined up. I pulled out all the stops tonight for my special lady.

I finished buttoning up my dress shirt and attaching my custom cufflinks before placing my Tom Ford suit jacket on. I stood in the floor length mirror checking out my fly ass suit and Ferragamo shoes, and a nigga was looking sharp if I did say so myself. My tailor had done a perfect job in fitting the suit to me, and I was impressed. Although my pops died while I was in my freshmen year of high school, he had always told me a real man and a boss should always have custom tailored or designed suits. A man should always dress for what he claimed and wanted to be. First impressions meant everything. It was a lifestyle, and I held that forever. No real boss was walking around in tees and Jordan's 24/7.

I was dressed to impress, but I was a street nigga at heart, so I placed my nine in the back of my pants and buttoned up my suit jacket. I sprayed on some Tom Ford cologne, snatched up my keys, phone, and wallet, and was on my way to meet up with Honour and the girls at his crib. I texted my Cairo that I was on my way to Honour's to scoop him and the girls, and that we should be to the venue in an hour tops. Cairo took the opportunity to help with this party and surprise engagement by being the first one there to make sure everything was in place and ready to go. I knew my brother though like the back of my hand, so I knew he had a motive for it. He had taken a liking to the event planner Prophecy, and that had him in the giving mood. I could never get my brother to be away from running the business for more than an hour, but lately, he was eager to help anytime it involved Prophecy.

My brother was feeling Prophecy hard, but she repeatedly shot down his attempts at getting close to her, and I laughed every time because he would be pissed, but that made him go harder and be more persistent. I tried to warn him to fall back, but he wasn't hearing me. Prophecy was damn near eight years older than Cairo, so she wasn't interested in him, and she made sure to let him know every time she blocked his shot. Prophecy was about her money, but I saw the way she looked at Cairo, and he may just be able to break her down, but it was gone be a challenge for sure, the cougars played no games.

I rode in silence to Honour's house just thinking about what I was about to do. I was excited but nervous at the same time. My stomach was in knots in anticipation of this whole thing. A part of me felt like something was about to pop off at the party, or something was going to go wrong. I tried my hardest to stay optimistic and positive about this night being one of the best that Sparkle and I ever had. I brushed the feelings off as much as I could and turned the music on. As Wale's "Black Bonnie" blasted through my car, I sparked my blunt and decided to ease my mind and just enjoy the evening of a lifetime. I was turning in my playboy lifestyle for the woman of my dreams.

Chapter Twenty-Two
CAIRO

"So, you not down with the whole cougar movement and shit, huh?" I asked, sipping my water while watching Prophecy closely as she continued to set up props and decorations while directing her staff on what to do as well.

"You are one persistent ass boy. Don't you have something else you should be doing besides wasting my time?" Prophecy spat, rolling her eyes at me and turning around to finish fixing the candy buffet table.

She began speaking into her earpiece to her staff in the back and security at the doors. Prophecy was about her business, and I loved that shit, but I could tell it was more layers to her. She had this hard-ass exterior, and I knew it was more than what meets the eye and me being the type of nigga I was, I could easily read that. Shorty had most definitely been through some things, and it was a story I was interested in learning. I wanted to know her, and I was gone to make that happen.

"I'm far from a boy, shawty. Don't let the baby face fool you, and I know you already know that. I saw you eyeing me up when I first walked in carrying all them boxes of liquor in here. Them gray sweats matter, huh man? Don't worry though as soon as ready for a real nigga I'ma bless your fine ass with all this wood. First, we have to get that attitude in check. This D is a gift, and you only get rewarded for good behavior," I replied confidently before walking up on her. She was holding her breath as I invaded her space. I stared down into her eyes, hovering over her closely. I winked at her and stepped around her, leaving her ass stuck. I had to get ready for the party, but I'd see her later tonight.

Once I reached my car, I looked back to see Prophecy still standing in the same spot I left her in staring at me intensely biting her bottom lip deep in thought. I blew her a kiss breaking her trance, and she rolled her eyes and flipped me the bird. All I could do was laugh and shake my head at lil mama. She was something else, but I was up for the challenge. She sparked something in me, and I had to have her. I watched her ass switch away until that thang she was toting around was no longer in my peripheral. I think I done messed around and found my future wife. I raced down the road to the hotel to get ready. Just as I was getting out of the car, my cell phone rang.

"What's good, bro?" I asked Pharaoh as I pulled into a parking spot.

I hopped out and walked in and caught the elevator just in time. I got off at my suite, and I placed the phone in between my ear and shoulder as fumbled around for my room key. I located the key card and swiped it on the door handled. The light turned green, and the door unlocked. I walked in, kicking the door closed behind me.

"Was everything good and in order at the venue? Is shit in place and all set?" Pharaoh rambled on with music playing loudly in the back.

"Bro, relax. Your baby bro got you. I got shit under control, and all handled on this end. You just get your girl here, and we got everything lined up and ready to go. But check this out big bro, I think your boy done got hit by cupid and shit. You and Honour shit is rubbing off on my ass," I said, laughing as I unzipped my garment bag that held my Hugo Boss suit for the evening.

"Man, I knew your ass was too eager to help and shit. Volunteering like you was doing me a favor and the whole time you just wanted to be up under Prophecy's ass. Don't run my event planner off. I need her for the wedding and shit, man." He laughed, clowning on me.

"Man, I'll change all that shit. I was saying about settling down for her ass. She feisty as hell but she independent a straight boss for sure. She is playing my ass to the left hard, but I caught her ass eyeing me up in my gray sweats this afternoon, so I know she's feeling the kid. It's just gone take a little more work than what I'm used to, but she worth the trouble," I boasted as I placed the phone on speaker so that I could gather my things and shower. I was pressed for time fooling around with Prophecy, and now shooting the shit on this phone with my bro.

"Yo, bro, be easy on Prophecy. Don't scare her ass off before my proposal!" he yelled into the phone while laughing.

"Hell nah, I'm about to lock her fine ass down, and I expect a thank you when I secure her as y'all wedding planner too, nigga," I replied now laughing with his ass.

We ended the call, and I showered thinking about Prophecy the whole time. Her name alone had my interest piqued. It's been a long time since I been this interested in a female, and especially for more than sex. Prophecy had come in and changed the game up on my ass, but I was playing for keeps in this game.

Chapter Twenty-Three

TREASURE

I was excited as hell for Sparkle's birthday celebration. We had been out all day getting ready. I paid for our hair and nails as my gift to her, and our men supplied their black cards for our outfits. We pulled out all the stops for this night. We had gotten Brazilian waxes for the first time, and after the pain subsided, I was geeked about the results. After studying so many YouTube tutorials and Pinterest posts, I did makeup well for an amateur, so I purchased us the complete Fenty line, and once we arrived home, I would beat our faces to the gods.

Honour texted me the whole time asking when I would be back, and I thought it was so cute because I was dying to be back in his presence as well. Honour had Pharaoh at the house with him, and they were awaiting our arrival. Honour had loaned me his Lexus truck to get around in whenever I needed to. The ride was so smooth, and the seats were everything. The scent of his cologne lingered in the air throughout the truck, making me feel at peace with thoughts of him.

"I have never had a birthday party in all my twenty-six years of life," Sparkle blurted out as we rode on the highway. She had been looking out the window most of the ride before she had just broken the silence with that statement.

"You didn't have a birthday party as a kid?" I asked a bit shocked by that. Didn't everyone at least have a hood birthday party with a home-made cake, the Neapolitan ice cream, Little Hugs drinks and Oscar Meyer hot dogs with chips?

"Nope, not at all. My mama was an only child and basically raised herself since she was fourteen. The only family she had was far out of town, so it was just us. I never met my father's family. For sixteen years, it was just mama and me until- well, never mind. There's no need to dwell on that and put a damper on the mood. I'm so happy to have my first party thanks to Pharaoh, and I'm glad for friends like you and Honour. I feel like I have a family, and that means a lot to me," Sparkle said, smiling nervously at me before turning back to the window.

I didn't press the issue, but I was definitely curious about her life. Come to think of it Sparkle never really spoke on her past life that much. She mentioned a bad relationship prior to our meeting, but that was it. In all actuality, I didn't know her as well as I thought. Nevertheless, she felt like a sister, and she was my best friend. I guess her past was too painful to discuss, so I would let her tell me when and if she decided to tell me.

We rode the rest of the way in silence lost in our thoughts while letting Nipsey Hussle's *Victory Lap* album play with no skips. After about fifteen minutes, we pulled into the subdivision and then into Honour's garage. I had used the gate key and garage remote with ease as if I had been living here for more than a few months. It was weird, but I felt at home and comfortable with Honour. He was always reminding me to just live and let everything flow. Nothing was rushed or felt forced with our relationship. Honour's exact words to me were to let our love be great and stop trying to block it.

I had only been out for a few hours but hurried inside as if I'd been away for days. I opened the door and got a whiff of Honour's cologne mixed with the smell of Kush. Honour knew I loved the way that Sauvage cologne smelled on him. It was my favorite scent he had. The true essence of a real man is the way they carry themselves. A man will be clean cut, sharp, smell good, and not walking around like a dirty nail nigga. Honour kept himself well-groomed, and his hygiene was a priority.

I had never seen him look scruffy, scraggly, or go around in the same clothes and draws for days at a time. I hated when Shyne acted as if he was so busy grinding on the street that he couldn't wash his ass and change his draws. I had a real grown ass man on my hands, and I loved it. I followed the scent to the master bedroom where I found him putting on his cufflinks. I hugged him from behind staring at us in the mirror. We looked damn good together, and I never wanted to leave his side. He winked at me and then turned and towards me placing a kiss on my cheek, and I headed off to shower so that I could do Sparkle and my makeup.

After completing our makeup looks and applying our lashes, we were ready to get dressed. I slid my pink shiny Fashion Nova dress on and slipped on my crystal embellished Betsy Johnson heels and was loving the outfit. My sew-in was popping with the body wave bundles. I did a light beat to my face but did a glitter pink eyeshadow to bring out my dress. I wore pink gloss on my lips and had the perfect crystal dangling earrings to match. I grabbed my clutch and headed to the front to take a few shots with fellas and get the party started.

Chapter Twenty-Four

SPARKLE

I stood admiring my newly highlighted tresses as I put my final touches on my outfit. I wore a pastel pink mini dress from Fashion Nova, and I had these strappy pink heels I found at Macy's to set the outfit off. The outfit was simple but sexy. With my bone straight hair parted down the middle, and my makeup complimenting my natural features, I was pleased with my birthday look. I walked out of the bathroom into the guest bedroom of Honour's home where Pharaoh was seated at the edge of the bed, looking like a snack patiently waiting on me. I stood directly in front of him and lifted my leg, placing my foot in between his legs on the edge of the bed.

"Can you fasten my straps for me?" I lovingly asked while watching him as his eyes roamed all over me looking me up and down. He didn't speak. He just proceeded to fasten my shoe straps. Once he finished, I switched to my next foot for him to do the same with. I was all dressed and ready to go. I grabbed my silver Gucci clutch bag and walked out the room with Pharaoh following close behind me making whistling noises, which caused me to put a little extra pep in my step, switching my hips and letting him pump me up like I was the shit.

"If we ain't have over a hundred people waiting on us to arrive, I'd bend your ass over right now," he said, biting into his bottom lip and slapping me on the ass.

I loved the way he adored me and looked at me as if I was irresistible to him. Pharaoh made me feel like I was the most beautiful girl in the world to him. I always had his undivided attention when we were together, and that was rare with men these days. They were always in their phone or focused on a TV. I was head over heels in love with this man, and I wasn't the least bit scared. Despite how quickly things took off with us, they just felt right. It had only been a few short months, but it felt like long years that I'd been with him, and I couldn't imagine not having him now.

Now that I was living with him, he had started to talk more about us buying a larger home together and starting a family. This last week alone he had been hinting to starting a family more and more each day. My heart wanted those things, but I cringed when I thought of who I really was and the way I had gone about everything with him.

Eventually, I would have to explain my past to him and let him know who I really was. I had to do this before it all blew up in my face one day. With Goose still out there only god knows where, I always felt uneasy, and the paranoia came in waves. I had prayed that after moving from my apartment, he was off my trail and had gone on with his life, but I knew Goose well enough to know he would search high and low for me until he found me. For all I know, he could be lurking in the shadows right now just waiting for the right time to come in and ruin the life I had and grown to love. My gun range visits were going well, and I went every week while taking self-defense classes two nights a week.

I felt freer and in control of my life each time I shot that gun at the target or I took down my instructor with a new move. My confidence with taking Goose down if I ever had to was high, and I was proud of myself for not running away to another city. I had my bestie and my man and his family. We were a family, and I love it and will fight and do what I could to keep it. I was ready to stop with the lies of who I was, and about where I was going each time, I went to gun practice or self-defense class. I had told Treasure and Pharaoh I was going to fitness classes at the gym.

We had stopped in the hallway at the mirror, and I relished in the feeling of being wrapped in Pharaoh's arms. He released me and fumbled around behind me, and I watched as he placed a diamond teardrop necklace around my neck. He kissed my neck, and that caused goosebumps to pop up all over my body. He grabbed my hand, leading me down the spiral staircase. We headed out the front door to the Vintage Rolls Royce parked in the horseshoe driveway. Honour and Treasure were already inside the car waiting on us. Honour drove with Treasure in the passenger seat, and Pharaoh and I hopped in the back and popped a bottle of Dom. I was on cloud nine, and I wished this night could last forever.

We sipped on the champagne and partied the whole ride to the party. The local radio station was playing some bomb ass mixes, and I was ready to get inside this party and turn all the way up. I was more than ready to see what all my man I had planned for me for my special day. Treasure was dancing in her seat having the time of her life right along with me. Who would have thought after the way Shyne broke her heart we would boss up and fall in love with some real ass men. Honour and Treasure were a good look. I loved how he protected her and made her happy. There was a rainbow at the end of our storms, and we deserved it.

Chapter Twenty-Five

GOOSE

We disguised ourselves as a part of the cleaning crew at this lavish ass party Pharaoh was throwing for Crystal. This bitch really thought she had got one over on me. I guess she took me for a sucka ass nigga that she could get one over on me. I was beyond ready to get back to Atlanta and away from this dumb ass nigga Shyne, and this airhead ass broad Rori. After the attempts to get Crystal at her apartment failed and she soon moved, my trail on her turned cold. That all changed last week when this business associate of Rori's hit her up about renting her Vintage Rolls Royce for a party. Rori sold and rented luxury vehicles at her dealership. That was like music to our ears because once she found out who the party was thrown by and for, we put our plan in motion.

I had on a dad hat, snapback type of hat pulled down low over my eyes as I removed trash from the props and decorations they had opened and set up. Guests were outside lining up for the doors to open ready to enter the event. Shyne was dressed the same as I was, but instead of black work sneakers, this nigga had on gold Nike Foamposites. This clown was forever doing some shit that would blow our plan up. However, the joke would soon be on him when Rori and I emptied our clips into him. Shyne was the type of nigga that wanted to be the boss but didn't know the first thing about being a boss and handling business. He was flashy and over the top and thought the world revolved around his whack ass.

Rori was running late damn near thirty minutes off the planned time to be here and ready. She had to retrieve her Vintage Rolls Royce, but I had yet to see or hear from her. I needed this shit to go smooth tonight. We had also planned to rob a few of the paid niggas in attendance. The plan was to split the profits three ways, but with Shyne about to be wiped out, it'll be split two ways. He wasn't to be trusted, and the way the Feds was breathing down his neck, I knew he would start throwing whoever he could under the bus, so he had to go, asap. The doors opened, and the crowd began to file inside, but the line was wrapped around the corner with people ready to enjoy all the free liquor and food that Pharaoh was offering.

Rori was still nowhere to be found. She was supposed to be mingling and finessing these niggas to dip off with her and then we would swoop in and corner them for whatever they had. I strolled through as if I was still cleaning and clearing out shit. I checked for Shyne and he was steady lusting after the bar girls and the party planner. The nigga's hat was halfway off, and he was sipping on a drink. He was a true fuck boy. Man, here he supposed to be keeping a low profile, and he is chasing pussy while on the mission. I needed him to point out to Rori who had the stash or cash that we needed.

I decided to get the shit popping on my own and do shit my way. Fuck Shyne and Rori at this point. I linked up with dumb and dumber trying to kill a few birds with one stone, but my daddy always said if you want something done right, do it yourself or beat that hoe's ass until she does it effortlessly. I had hoes making my money back home, and I only came out here to get my property. Crystal belonged to me, and I be dammed if she thought she would get the last laugh. After seeing how these niggas in Miami was living and making money, my plan went to the left. Now, I needed this come up, and my wife back where she belongs, and I'd be on my way.

I had grown tired of Shyne and Goose after all these weeks cooped up in the house with them both. Enough was enough, so I came up with a plan of my own. I had the pleasure of meeting Prophecy the dope ass event planner, and she inspired me to get back on my boss lady shit. It was time to remove these bitter ass men from my life and live my best life. Treasure and Sparkle had never done anything to me, and I realized my jealousy and insecurities played a big part in me helping Goose and dealing with Shyne for this long. Those women had never met me or done anything personally to me, but my jealousy for the way these men were all over them led me to partake in this messed up plot. I refused to lead them to these crazy ass scorned men. I don't blame Treasure for leaving Shyne, and shit, Goose was a coked out, abusive ass, pimp so Sparkle, Crystal, or whatever her name is did what she had to do, and I don't blame her one bit.

I had put a bug in the security guard Steel's ear about a possible threat to the girls. He said he'd be on it and thanked me for the heads up. I knew Steel from back in the day when I used to strip at KOD where he was a bouncer. He now had his own security business and provided bouncing and bodyguard service to people. For years, Steel tried to get at me, but I always avoided him. He treated me like I mattered, and he was kind and sweet to me, which I wasn't used to, so I played him to the left, and I was regretting that now. I could have been happily married with a house full of kids and real relationship goals out here.

I had been on the City Girls wave before the City Girls was even on it. I always lived as I pleased and never wore my heart on my sleeve. I had no emotions or feelings for any man out here. It was just sex and a good time with me. Then came Shyne with his sweet-talking slick ass and he got me to catch feelings. I also had a temporary moment of insanity but not any longer. I was ready to let love find me and live life to the fullest. I soon realized that Shyne wasn't shit and never gave a fuck about me other than getting in my bed. I was back as if I never left, and I'd be a force to be reckoned with in no time.

I tucked myself off to the side in an all-black truck waiting on the guys to arrive in the vintage car. I'd retrieve my car and be on my way back to the regularly scheduled program, and I hope that Steel handled Shyne and Goose before they could do anything to the girls. Steel had slipped me his business card, and I planned to hit him up on the personal cell number he wrote on the back for me.

As I waited, I felt relief knowing that my things were being moved to my new place that neither Shyne nor Goose knew about. I was no longer playing with them in these treacherous games, especially going against Honour and Pharaoh that was like suicide. The game was over.

Chapter Twenty-Seven

SPARKLE

W e pulled up to the party, and I couldn't believe all the people that were in attendance to celebrate my birthday. As soon as we stepped out the ride, a photographer was on snapping pictures left and right of us. We lined up like we were taking prom pictures right in front of the vintage car and posed for the camera. Just as we finished our little photo shoot, Honesty and Nile climbed out a limo with two fine guys trailing behind them. I remembered meeting Shaw at Honour's mama's house a while back, but I hadn't met the guy that Nile had with her, but I had an idea of who it was.

During our many girl's days, she had confided in me about her relationship with Compton. He was from California and one of the brothers of her and Honesty's roommate Cali from the summer program they did last year. I knew they were the reasons why the girls decided to go to LA for school. The girls hugged us all while the guys trailed slowly behind them not sure if they were welcomed.

I cleared the air by introducing myself to Compton and then everyone else. I felt how tense Pharaoh had become upon seeing them, and I squeezed his hand when I saw the veins in his neck pulsating, and his jaw clenched tightly together. He looked over at me and gave me a wink and half smile. He was so overprotective of Nile and

Honesty, and so were Honour and Cairo too. The poor girls had three crazy and overprotective men hovering over them and always on them about the choices they make. I constantly tried to tell him to back off some and let her live life. Nile was eighteen, and Pharaoh treated her like she was a twelve-year-old. The girls were both honor roll students and smart as hell.

Compton and Crenshaw were respectful and friendly, but I saw the bad boy in them, and the vibe was that they were true gangsters at heart. They were actually getting along with the guys and seemed to fit in with our circle. The girls were in love. It was all in their eyes and on their faces as they looked at the guys and talked to them, but those boys were in love too. I peeped how they handled the girls, and it was all love between them.

After making my way around meeting Pharaoh's friends and business associates, he introduced me to Prophecy, the lady responsible for planning me this glammed out bomb ass party. She was cool as hell and pretty. Once Cairo made his way over, she headed in the opposite direction, but he was quick on her tail. Pharaoh was clowning them both making me laugh with tears. Cairo was a mess yelling out cougar as he followed behind Prophecy.

The music was bumping, and we all danced and drank for hours. It was time to cut my cake. The cake was a three-tier cream and gold glittered blinged out cake with sparklers and candles adorning the top tier. Everyone started to sing happy birthday, and once the cake was in front of me, I closed my eyes and made a wish then blew out the candles, and everyone erupted with cheers and claps.

I turned to see Pharaoh holding a mic in his hand and asking everyone for their attention. He led me to the patio where fireworks were going off, and he pointed to the sky where a huge blimp was flying by. On the LED display of the blimp the words *Will You Marry Me?* was scrolling across. I was in shock, and I turned around to see Pharaoh down on one knee with the most beautiful engagement ring.

Before I could answer, or he could even speak someone began to clap loudly interrupting our moment. The clapping got closer, so Pharaoh stood to both feet searching for the culprit who was being rude. When a guy a janitor's jumpsuit with a hat pulled down low stepped forward through the crowd and removed the hat from his head, as he stepped closer, I almost fainted. He looked me directly in the eyes and smiled the most devious smile and then winking at me. Pharaoh looked beyond confused as he looked from him to me and back and forth a few times. Then I heard the voice that haunted many of my dreams and the basis of my paranoia. A voice I hated and thought I would never have to hear again spoke.

"Crystal, my beautiful, deceitful, ass wife, you're looking good for a dead woman," he said with so much malice and hate in his voice. He stared me down with an evil glare, now stepping right up on me.

The tears slowly fell, and my breathing became labored. I was beginning to hyperventilate and lose control as the devil himself, Goose, stood before me. He went to reach his hand towards my face, but Pharaoh knocked it away and stepped in front of me, blocking me from him.

"Yo my nigga, I'ma need you to back up out my woman's face. You got the wrong one partna, so back the hell up!" Pharaoh spoke through clenched teeth. I was scared shitless that things were about to go all wrong.

"Nah muthafucka, I got the right bitch. You got the wrong one. See, your girl Sparkle here done played your ass. This is my wife Crystal, who was supposed to be dead. My name is Goose, her husband, nice to meet you, my bad for ruining your goofy ass proposal!" Goose spat viciously.

Pharaoh turned and looked at me in disbelief and pure disgust. I felt my heart break as I saw the love that he had for me turn cold right before my eyes. I was frozen in place and couldn't move as I cried trying to find the words to say and explain what happened. We were locked in a stare down when a commotion broke out off in the distance. I could see Shyne and Cairo throwing blows as Honour was helping Treasure up from the floor. Before we could head that way, shots rang out, and Goose pulled a gun out, aiming it at me. Pharaoh threw a punch so hard for Goose's jaw that it caused him to lift up and fly into the patio furniture. Everyone was scrambling and running to get out of there.

Pharaoh snatched me up, and we took off running towards the

front of the venue. Shots were flying past us quickly, and as I looked back, I saw Goose shooting towards us. Pharaoh pulled his gun from his waistband and fired back. We reached the corner where he pushed me around it covering me as he shot back at Goose. A black truck with dark tinted windows pulled up, and the doors flew open. Security hopped out, Pharaoh pushed me towards them, and they tossed me in. Pharaoh gave me one last look shaking his head before running off towards the front door. I assumed he was going to check on Honour and Cairo. I screamed for him, but he kept going. The child lock was on, and I couldn't get out. It was chaos everywhere.

The driver's side passenger door swung open, and Honesty, Nile, Treasure, Prophecy, and a woman I didn't know were all thrown in one by one into the back seat. The door was barely closed when the car took off full speed ahead out the parking lot. We were all screaming and crying hysterically. The car was going so fast as we all held on tight to whatever we could trying to get a seat and snap our seatbelts. I needed to know where Pharaoh was, and I had no phone. Everything was left back at the pier.

"Sparkle, who the hell was that man? What the hell is going on? Who is Crystal?" Treasure was screaming question after question to me with tears running down her face.

"I am Crystal, and that man is Goose, my ex-husband. I faked my death about two years ago to get away from him. He was abusive, obsessive, and pretty soon, he would have ended up killing me. I thought I planned everything out perfectly to escape him when I fled Georgia. I had been under his control since I was sixteen when I met him, and we married right after my mother died when I was eighteen. I'm so sorry I didn't mean to get you all involve on my mess," I cried.

Treasure pulled me into her, and we hugged. Everyone else was sitting there with their mouths hanging open. However, before we could discuss things further, the car was rammed hard from the rear. Our driver Steel the security guard sped up going faster than we already were, but the car rammed us again sending the car spinning out of control. We all screamed, and my life flashed before my eyes before we crashed into another vehicle. I felt myself going forward and my head hit the window, and everything went to black.

Chapter Twenty-Eight
HONOUR

Everything happened so fast, but we were able to get the girls out safely and into the car with our security guard, Steel. We had some of the niggas on our team go snatch up Shyne and they took him to the warehouse, but we couldn't find that nigga Goose, and we searched the premises two times over before we got the fuck out of dodge. Once Cairo hopped in the driver seat of his ride, we were in route to the warehouse. I dialed up Steel repeatedly to check on the girls and make sure they were all ok, but I just got voicemail each time. I was growing more and more irritated each time his phone rang over to voicemail. Pharaoh was too damn quiet in the back. I knew he was pissed and his feelings, so I left him alone.

Cairo had snatched up the girl's belongings, so we had all their purses and cell phones and no way to call them directly. I tried Steel again and still got no answer. I banged my hand on the dashboard, pissed beyond control. My mind was racing a mile a minute as I tried to piece together why Sparkle/Crystal or whatever the fuck her name was would keep that info from Pharaoh. I wondered if Treasure knew any of the info, or were we all were just finding out.

I didn't take Sparkle to be a snake. Sis seemed solid as hell, so it had to be a good explanation for this whole situation. Pharaoh wasn't trying to hear that shit. I understood him though. He felt betrayed, and loyalty meant a lot to us.

We had Crenshaw and Compton in the car with us and they were quiet too. Them little niggas surprised the hell out of me because they were right with us fucking niggas up and bussing their guns. They were official as hell with the gunplay, and I was shocked how they had our backs. I received the information back last night from the PI on these cats. I was in for a surprise when he told me that the OG Caution from Compton, a gangster ass blood, was their father. They had a sister name Cali that was close with Honesty and Nile. She was roommates with the girls last summer when they stayed in LA for a summer program earning college credits.

I never wanted my sister and little cousin to date a street nigga, and damn sure not no Crip or blood gangbangers, but in the situation that we were in tonight and with how they handled that shit, I felt secure in knowing they would protect Honesty and Nile at all cost. Tonight they proved they were ten toes down for our little sisters. I was going against my initial decision to shut them all the way down, but I gave in and was gone let them rock and live they life. I now knew that Compton and Crenshaw was some true gangster that would ride for their girls, our sisters.

Chapter Twenty-Nine

PHARAOH

I sat back chilling in deep thought in the corner of the warehouse zoning out. I briefly tuned in as Honour commenced to beating the shit out of Shyne. I was sipping on a bottle of D'usse trying to drown out my inner thoughts. A nigga was hurting, and I was livid as hell. Sparkle wasn't who she had claimed to be, and that was burning me up. Shorty could have kept shit real with me the way I kept it all the way real with her. I was always a hundred with her, and yet she wasn't even the person I knew her to be this whole time. I was ready to marry her, start a family, and build our foundation. It was all a lie.

I let her slide on discussing her past with me because it appeared to bother and hurt her. I wanted to be patient and understanding with her, so I never pressed the issue, but never did I think it was because she was hiding whole secret life and identity. This entire fucking time she was playing my ass. I needed answers like yesterday from her because this shit wasn't making any type of sense to me, and she was the only one who could make it make sense. Shorty wasn't after my money, so I scrapped that theory and was drawing all blanks on what her angle and intentions were. I can't see this whole thing being a plot because they never intended to meet us, so that was out too.

"Yo, Cairo, where the fuck is this nigga Steel at?" I yelled out in frustration, pounding my fist into the table next to me. I was pissed the hell off and needed to see Sparkle immediately. She owed me a hell of an explanation about her disloyalty.

"Man, bro, I don't even know. This nigga isn't answering the phone. I hit up his brother Stone too, and he isn't answering his phone either. I'm starting to think something is up," he replied, looking just as stressed as I do.

I got up to go question Shyne, and there was a knock at the warehouse door. I pulled my strap out and eased to the door. I asked for a name, and they yelled back Stone. I quickly pulled the door up, and Stone looked stressed out.

"We got a problem," he stated, stepping in and allowing me to slam the door back down and latch it back up.

"What the fuck are you talking about we have a problem. Where the hell is Steel? He was supposed to meet us here with the girls!" I roared at the top of my lungs, losing all patience I had left, not caring that spit was flying from my mouth as I spoke.

"That's the problem I'm talking about. I don't know where they are. I tracked the GPS of the truck to the highway, and when I arrived there, it had been involved in a crash, but the police said no one was at the scene when they arrived except for the other vehicle's passengers and driver. I been searching everywhere and calling Steel's phone, and he is not picking up," Stone replied with a worried somber expression on his face.

Everyone had heard what he had just told me, and we all were stuck with no real solution. I paced back and forth, trying to think how we were going to find them.

"Georrgiaa," Shyne said barely above a whisper while coughing and spitting up blood and groaning out in pain.

I marched over to him snatching him up by the collar of his jumpsuit, lifting his upper body close to me so that we were face to face.

"Tell us what the hell you know and where the girls could be?" I yelled before dropping him back down to the ground. He fell back onto his back rolling over onto his knees, coughing some more.

"Goose is a pimp out in Georgia... urrgghhh, and he got a team of niggas that he had come up here yesterday to Miami, and they probably plotted against all of us and took the girls back to Georgia," he said in between coughing still and wincing in pain.

Honour was already making phone calls to get reinforcement for this ride out to Georgia. We kept Shyne alive a little longer, putting him in cuffs and tossing him in the back of the truck. We all piled up into two trucks with heavy artillery ready for war. We hopped in traffic and on the interstate heading to take Goose and anyone else he had with him out once and for all. We were getting the ladies back safe and in one piece if it was the last thing we did.

I don't know who I fell in love with, but I was going to get her back, fuck it. We'll figure out who the hell she was and what she wanted after I got her back home where she belonged.

To Be Continued

SNEAK PEEK

Please Me: An Urban Erotica

P**lease is to afford or give pleasure or satisfaction.**
        Kaienne is a hardworking woman and has always been about business. But years of work and no play has turned her into what some consider a bitter sex deprived B*tch. Being the Boss and running a successful Real Estate company comes with pros and cons. The cons seem to be rolling in with ease as the pros are now few and far in between that is until JaCruz "Cru" Campbell walks into her office with his Ego not far behind. He is instantly attracted to the woman who appears to be tougher than what she actually is.

After the embarrassment and hurt that her ex caused Kaienne has focused all her energy into her business and projects becoming celibate not by choice. Kaienne allows Cru to open her eyes and mind up to new desires and sexual adventures she never thought to experience. When feelings develop beyond the bedroom will Cru take the opportunity to finally love one woman or will a scandal shatter any real chances at love.

Follow these lovers as they embark on a journey of pleasure, pain, and ecstasy in the drama filled pages of Please Me!

PROLOGUE

I quickly threw everything off my desk and into my briefcase. I snatched up my purse and cell phone before heading to the door. I turned the lights out rushing out the door and to my car. I hopped in and hit the push to start button, quickly throwing my car in reverse. I briefly checked my surroundings on the backup camera before I slammed my now shoeless foot on the gas. I sped out the parking lot racing to get to Bilal's favorite bakery. I was beating my own ass because I worked late last night and left early this morning before Bilal woke up to get into work and hit the gym before starting my busy workday. I was a horrible wife and felt like shit. What wife forgets her man's birthday?

Today was Bilal's 30th birthday, and I forgot all about it. I only remembered after my assistant stated he could go pick up the cake if I needed him too. Every year I get the same butter almond and fresh strawberry cake for Bilal's birthday just as he does for mine because it was both of our favorite cake. I arrived at the bakery parking crooked and hopped out running in barefoot without a care leaving my car running. I waved to Nellie, the baker, who has made every special cake for us from our wedding to birthdays and on. She met me around the counter with the cake, and I was back out the door again racing to my car. I sped out the lot in route to Bilal's office.

Bilal owned an architect firm and a few other businesses but building and designing was his core focus. We worked our way through college together both starting our own businesses by twenty-five and our five-year plan and five years married were good for the most part, except I still hadn't given Bilal the babies that he wanted. I was supposed to grind and build my realty firm for two years and then grind to be the top realty company. At twenty-nine, I'd done just that and then some, but no kids yet. We weren't not trying, but we barely had sex to even procreate. I arrived at Bilal's office and noticed only his car and one other in the lot. I hopped out, grabbing the cake, kicking the door closed with my bare feet and heading in. My feet were still sore from running around the office in meeting after meeting on my feet in six-inch heels.

The door was locked, so I knocked a few times but received no answer. That was strange and struck something in me to make me feel like something was off. My woman's intuition was at an all-time high, I guess you could say. I used my spare key and opened the door. It was quiet, but I instantly became alert at the sounds of moans. I followed the sounds down the hall to Bilal's office. The door was crack, just enough leaving a small enough opening where I could see through it, and I could see a naked Bilal standing up moving his pelvis in an in and out motion. I had reached the door finally quickly pushing it open. My heart raced out my chest as my stomach did flips and drops. They never even moved because they were too wrapped up in the sex they were having. My body felt hot all over and the anger was swiftly rising within me.

I launched the box containing the cake at them, and the cake and frosting splattered all over them.

Bilal was fucking his secretary on his desk in his office with no condom on. I backed away from them as he tried to near me with his raw dick just swinging about as he walked. I was mortified and disgusted at the sight before me. This was husband, but right now I didn't know who this man was because the man I married would never do this to me or so I always thought. I felt my body becoming hot all over, and the tears were building and ready to flow like the Falls. But, before my tears could fall the smirk and laugh that escaped from Laya's mouth stopped us both. He turned with the quickness while my head whipped towards her direction no longer staring at Bilal. This bitch wore a smirk while running her hand over her small round belly. She was still on top of the desk with her wrap dress opened, showing off her perfect, braless breasts.

I charged towards her, but Bilal snatched me up before I could make contact. That infuriated me sending me into full rage mode as I rained down punches and kicks all over him. I was getting good hits in until I felt my hair being snatched pulling me backwards, causing me to fall and land in the mess of cake on the floor. Bilal had gotten Laya to let my hair go and then hurried her out the door, locking it once she was out the door. She began to kick and scream obscenities at both us, but more so to me. The last part I heard was she was six months pregnant with Bilal's son before I let the tsunami of tears and cries release that I was holding on to. Bilal pulled me up, but I snatched away from him and helped myself up.

"Why would you do this to me, to us?" I screamed at him.

"Don't act like this is a shocker, Kaienne. You are never around. I feel like a damn worker or client of yours having to be penciled into your schedule. I talk to your damn assistant more than I talk to you. I'd told you for years that I was ready for a family, and you pushed work and success over me. I never set out to fall out of love with you, but it happened, and I'm in love with Laya. She gets me and has been here for me. She and I are going to marry once our divorce is final. I hate that you had to find out this way. I planned to tell you over dinner and give you the divorce papers. I will pay you alimony, and you can keep everything. I just want to cut our ties, dissolve all joint accounts, and liquidate all assets so that I can move on with life. My family deserves that," he replied unfazed by my anger and hurt.

He looked at me with pity and disgust that sent a chill up my spine with each word he spoke. I was crushed at his words, and all I could do was gather my things and walk out. I had to get as far away from there and him as possible. When I hopped in my car, I didn't even have a destination I just knew I couldn't go home. It wasn't even home anymore. It was just a house of lies, secrets, and hurt.

I drove to my big sister Kaielle's home almost an hour away from me in Jersey. I knew it was late, but I needed her. We weren't as close as we once were, but we still FaceTimed and talked often. I pulled into her driveway and hopped out still barefoot from earlier, clothes covered in cake, hair a disheveled mess, and mascara smudged and running down my face.

I rang the bell waving at the camera above the door that I knew was there since I recommended it when I sold her and her husband Wood purchased the home. I could hear little voices and the pitter-patter of small feet getting closer to the door. The locks were undone and the door cam open and there stood my sister looking shocked to see me. Once she took in my appearance, her expression changed to concern in a snap, and she pulled me inside, shutting the door and locking it before arming the security system again.

Kaielle was paranoid all our lives, but when she married Wood, she became even more paranoid. Wood had dealings deep in the mafia due to his family lineage and generations of mafia bosses.

"Girls go in the playroom and give Auntie Enne and me a minute to talk," she sweetly said to my nieces Amerie and Kima. They shook their curly heads and took off running towards the back of the home.

"What the hell happened to you, Kaienne?" Kaielle said as she pulled out a barstool for me to sit and she sat next to me.

"Bilal left me for his secretary. She is six months pregnant with their son." My voice cracked, and my hands trembled as I spoke the truth out loud.

"WHATTTTT! Oh my god, Kaienne, I'm so sorry!" she gasped and then pulled me into her, allowing me to cry out my heart on her shoulders.

I always prided myself on being a strong woman that could get through anything, but I had no idea how I would ever get through this. My cries weren't helping to erase the pain, and I felt my heart turning to ice. I despised Bilal, and I believed that all men would cheat. You can be a successful woman who brings home just as much if not more money than the man of the house, and instead of respecting and cherishing that, they will feel threatened by that. I never felt bad about myself or the success I had, but tonight, right now at this very moment, I questioned if I was truly good enough to have the man the career and a family. I never wanted to be the single, lonely, successful woman. I wanted it all, and I thought I'd have that with Bilal, but all I have left is myself and my career.

Kaielle took me to the guest bedroom and gave me clean night-clothes and towels to shower. I was sticky, and my feet were a hot dirty mess from being barefoot, but none of that compared to the way my soul hurt. I was hurt to the core of my heart, and the more hurt I felt and tears I cried, the angrier I became. I showered and attempted to wash away all the pain and hurt of today's events, but it was no use. The moment I laid in that bed, the pain and reality of my life hit me full force and sent me back to that crying spell. I cried as I thought of all the years I shared with Bilal and all the dreams and secrets I poured out to him.

I racked my brain, giving myself a major headache trying to figure out when things shifted for us. I know we have been hot and cold in the sex department, but I never thought it was because he was falling out of love with me and in love with another woman. The cheating a woman can get past when it means nothing but a nut, but when that man loves the woman he cheated with and gives her his seed to create a family, that's a different level. The cheating hurts but the baby and no longer loving me crushed me.

I deactivated all my social media only keeping the business pages that my assistant ran on the daily. I changed my phone number and powered off my phone. I needed to rest and start my new life, but first I needed to cry the hurt out and deal with this heartbreaking blow. I had to release all that I was feeling so I could let the hurt go. I told myself all the things that I could to stay positive and myself but my heart turned to ice that day and a coldhearted bitch was born.

Kaienne
One Year Later
I walked into the office, and everyone scattered as I made my way

to the reception desk. I had a new rich client coming into the office
and had no time to play. I looked down over the brim of my sunglasses
as the receptionist, Tara, skimmed through a wedding magazine. She
hadn't noticed me yet, and I was growing impatient. I waited another
second as she circled a dress that was hideous before I banged my fist
on the top of the reception desk, causing a picture frame to bounce
and fall hitting her in the head.

She jumped and looked up, locking eye with me frightened as if she
was staring in the face of the devil. I rolled my eyes and stuck my hand
out, waiting for my mail and messages. She quickly gathered up what
was mine and placed it into my hand. I took notice of the small
wedding ring that barely held a chip of a diamond and set in a silver
band. I would never accept that Cracker Jack box of a ring, and neither
should she, but not all women knew their worth and full potential. I
decided to enlighten this little girl and hope she took heed to my
advice as it would save her from years wasted to only end up heart-
broken and damaged at the hands of a worthless man.

"Sweetie, let me drop a little knowledge on you. In no time in life
should a man be asking to marry you if he has no financial means or
stability to support and take care of a family. Have your own bag, but
he better be able to hold his own too. That ring is a reflection of what
he thinks of you. Does he think so low and small of you that he
couldn't pick out a ring that matches the love and beauty of what you
two shares? I'd reconsider planning a wedding just yet boo." I winked
at her, retrieved my things, and made my way to my office.

As I walked to my office, everyone parted like the Red Sea as I
made my way past them. I stopped by my assistant Vell's office, and he
was nowhere to be found. He had been my assistant since I started this
company, but his ass was skating on thin ice around here lately with all
his mishaps.

I met Vell during an internship at a local newspaper company, and
we clicked becoming besties instantly. Nevertheless, after the way I
was betrayed and played, I took no shit from anyone anymore, not
even my bossy ass mama. I paged Vell over the loudspeaker to meet me
in the conference room. I wanted to go over the agenda for today's
meeting. I had a guy by the name of JaCruz "Cru" Campbell coming in.

He was a successful business owner here in New York. He owned a long list of businesses and was interested in property to expand as well as a personal home for his permanent stay now that he was an official citizen. He was from Jamaica and had been here in the states for some time now. Cru had a very public divorce with a supermodel from the U.S., which was rumored to be solely for his citizenship.

I wasn't one to judge, especially when money was involved. I read the things that were said in the blogs and on social media about him, but I would take the opportunity to be the judge of that. In this real estate business, you had to remove the personal feelings, or you'd never make a dime. I may not care for someone, but that doesn't mean I can't do my job and find them a property and seal a deal. I'd done it numerous times for men and women that I didn't care for or particularly like, but as the saying goes, money talks and bullshit walks. I stood at the huge picture window of the conference room just taking in the view. I heard the huge frosted glass doors open and close. I knew from the cologne that it was Vell.

"You have been slacking off big time, and if you can't handle being my assistant, then turn in your notice and save me the stress of having to let your ass go," I stated with my back to him still staring out at Times Square.

"Girllll bye, yo ass needs me. Now, let's get to the order of business. Cru and his team of people will be arriving in approximately thirty minutes. I have all of the requested refreshments from KC's deli already here, and Stacy will be in to set that up any minute. Next on the list is your finalization on the divorce. It appears that Bilal has finally agreed to your terms and will relinquish all rights to the properties and assets. However, he did state his business account is not up to split since he started that on his own. The last order of business is Dante. He is adamant that you work on finding his next bar location and not Seven. I believe it's a matter of Seven and him having crossed that very thin line between business and pleasure.

I don't know how you didn't drop that girl after the last client she decided to drop her draws for, but anyway, that's your business partner and just my opinion. Oh, and the PowerPoint is already loaded and ready to run once Cru arrives," he replied all in one breath never missing a beat and giving me the time to collect myself before I lose my cool.

"Vell, do you take me as your boss as a joke? What is it that you are on? It's crack. It has to be crack because who in their right mind would dismiss their boss in the manner that you just did. Nothing about what I asked you was a damn joke, and yet you carry on with your *girl bye* or whatever the hell you say as if I am not trying to run a damn business. I am your boss first and foremost and don't forget that," I stated now standing directly in his face.

"Well, boss lady, ma'am I apologize geesh. You really need to get off the celibacy train because this time with no D has your ass walking around with your panties in a bunch, and a stick up your ass. Instead of this high horse that you rode in on, how about you find a stiff dick instead. I'll see you in twenty for the meeting, and I'll make sure to pour a shot of Hennessey in your coffee," he replied, doing a dramatic ass about face and leaving out.

All I could do was shake my head at him, but I laughed to myself because Vell was a character, and I loved him. I knew I'd become a bit tougher and stern with the people in my life and especially at work. I felt that after the shit that Bilal pulled over my eyes and left me broken and lost, I needed to build myself up stronger so no one could cross me ever again. I wouldn't say I wasn't dreaming of some good back-breaking sex, but business had become my only focus, and it helped me get through the toughest time in my life. I could admit I was cranky, and maybe I needed to loosen up, but I wasn't about to hop on the next dick I came across, so I guess I needed to get me a toy. I hadn't even pleasured myself in over a year let alone got some D as Vell would say. I had no desire for love or sex. I'd lost all interest after Bilal.

The image of him fucking his secretary, well actually making love to her, was an image that I'd fought to forget. He was so into her and pleasing her body and the look of satisfaction on his face was one I'd never witnessed. Mentally the whole ordeal had scarred me badly, and I was still trying to pick up my face off the floor of his office and recover from the tragic loss. I placed my whole heart and life in his hands, and he fumbled it like he was a toddler catching a football for the first time. My mind had been focusing on so many other things since then to try and stay afloat, but I was drowning and sinking fast. I knew I had to find peace and happiness again because being labeled as a bitter bitch was a title that I'd never associate myself with, but this point in life I'd become exactly that.

৪

I sat at the head of the long rectangular table and waited for Mr. Campbell to be bought in. Vell walked in followed by two big buff bodyguards dressed in all black and sunglasses. It was a sunny day for May, so I didn't bother with why they still had the shades on inside the building. In walked JaCruz "Cru" Campbell immediately after and another guy noticeably shorter than Cru. I stood to greet them, and Cru pulled my hand into his kissing the back of my hand softly while looking into my eyes. I wore a nervous smile quickly pulling my hand back and taking my seat. I was a little thrown off because his ass appeared to be so corny on TV and in the media, but the vibe I got in person was the complete opposite.

I was feeling a little hot, and my throat felt dry as the desert. I signaled for Vell, and he quickly handed me my bottle of Fiji water and sat the cup of coffee in front of me while giving me a smirk and a side eye. I ignored his glares and focused on the matter at hand. I took a sip of my water and waited as the guys passed around the refreshments. I caught the glances from the short guy and the intense stare of Cru. The man was fine as hell and that had me a little off my square. I wasn't expecting to be attracted to him in the least bit, but my body was on fire with thoughts of him circling my brain.

I tried to regain my composure as quickly as possible to get this meeting moving along. I was hoping that by the end of this meeting he'd be signing on the dotted line for a lucrative building deal.

"Welcome everyone, and thank you for your time today. I will show you a presentation of some of the business I have helped get off the ground through my building program and then open up the floor for any questions or concerns before we discuss numbers and negotiations," I stated as I stood up and pointed my remote at the projector to drop the screen and begin the presentation.

The projector came down, and the show began. I watched as they nodded their heads in approval, and their eyes held a look of surprise and intrigue as each business my building program helped build from the ground up. When the slides stopped, I allowed the questions, and they had plenty to go around. The program offered the opportunity to rent to own a building that would be designed and transformed to house the business they had plans for. All cost of the remodeling and hiring and staffing was funded through the project and paid off with a nice down payment and monthly payments for a short period of time with a low-interest rate. I cut out the bank and middleman and provide that option directly.

Cru expressed that he was most definitely interested and signed on for his two clubs to be under my building program. The next order of business was to take him out to look at a few properties for purchase. I concluded the meeting and stood to shake all their hands. As the guards exited, Cru stayed seated, and his short friend stood at the door attempting to give me googly eyes. I ignored him and cleared my throat for Vell and Stacy to see him out and leave Cru and me to discuss a few details about his home interests and needs. The short friend wasn't getting the picture though, and instead of seeing his way out, he walked towards me. I looked from Cru to him, and he wore the same confused look as me.

"Aye yo, ma, let me take you to lunch?" The short man asked boldly.

"Excuse me? I am not your ma, and I am not interested. You need to learn manners and the way to approach a woman. I am not one of the girls you are used to. Have a nice day and please leave Mr. Campbell and me to handle grown folks' business," I stated, cutting my eyes to Vell. He politely led the way for Short man out the door.

"I apologize about my assistant. He was out of line, and I will be sure to speak with him about that. Now, back to this grown folks business, I'd like to see the lofts in Manhattan Beach that you have available and in the SoHo district as well. As for tomorrow's meeting, I have reservations booked at Ruth Chris at seven p.m. See you then, beautiful," he said while giving me that intense stare down again.

I couldn't even speak. I just sat back and watched him excuse himself from the conference room. I don't cross the lines of business and pleasure, but for Mr. Campbell, I was entertaining the possibility. His lips and that voice had left me wanting to continue sitting in his presence, and the authority he possessed caused a river to flow in the once dry and cobwebbed over desert in my pencil skirt.

I hurried to my office and to the bathroom to clean myself up and get ready for my next order of business. Finally, I'd be free from this drawn out divorce with Bilal. You would think after he had left me that he wouldn't put up a fight over the assets, but leave it up to Bilal to shock me with his claim of abandonment as the reason he found love in another woman.

I was over this whole ordeal, but I refused to let him get off with hurting me and walking away with half of my hard works pay. He accepted my final offer, and he could keep all funds from his own business, but he wouldn't get a dime of my money or any of the assets. I would say my offer was fair considering what he had done. Once we signed on those dotted lines today, I had plans to let myself live freely.

I wanted to live the life that Nola Darling lived on *She's Gotta Have It*. Nola lived her life unapologetically with no care or concern of what anyone might think. She had men falling at her feet and women too. She did what she loved to do and had friends to hang and spend time with. I needed that life and to feel alive again. This last year has caused me to feel so dead and empty, and I refuse to live another day that way.

x

"For this business dinner you sure are getting extra sexy, Ms. Kaienne," Vell stated, snapping his fingers.

"You got some nerve after you practically called me a desperate bitch who needed some dick in her life," I replied, laughing at his extra ass.

I chose to wear a white bandage off the shoulder dress and these spiral wrap around the ankle and leg silver and rhinestone heeled sandals. I let my hair fall naturally and wild. With some gloss and light pink eye shadow, I was ready to go. I felt sexy, and in fact, I felt the sexiest that I had ever felt. I checked my Uber app, and my ride was arriving. I grabbed my house keys and my Fendi crossbody chained bag and made my way out the house.

"Don't wait up!" I yelled to Vell my assistant turned temporary roommate.

I hopped in the Uber and made my way to some new low-key lounge that Cru invited me to. I was tied up in meetings all day, so I'd missed our Reservations at Ruth Chris and Cru refused to take no for an answer so here I was on my way to meet him. I tried to get some reviews on this lounge, but it appeared to be not one. That was odd but I figured it was some celebrity secret spot that I'd hadn't been put on to. I was nervous, but deep down, I was excited to see him. His smile was infectious, and he had the body of a Greek god. I preferred not to mix business with pleasure, but the way my body reacted to his presence, it was a craving that I had to feed. I was freeing myself and celebrating the new single and free Kaienne.

I sat lingering in the Uber hands sweating and head spinning as I stared at the lounge. I wanted to get out and do as I had convinced myself too, but my nerves were shot, and I was second-guessing this night. The Uber driver cleared his throat, and I hurried out the car. He sped off quickly, making my decision for me. I made my way slowly to the front of the lounge. Here it goes I pepped talked myself and in I went.

I searched the front bar area and saw no sign of Cru, but I was approached by a hostess who led me towards a set of stairs. I followed her up the stairs where the music slowly faded the higher up we went. We reached the top, and she pushed a silk curtain to the side, letting me in. I walked in and was taken aback by the romantic scene. There were candles lit, and Maxwell played softly in the distance. Cru stood from the table to meet me halfway. He took my hand kissing the back of it, which sent feelings all through my body I had never felt not even with Bilal. I smiled at him and felt a layer of my tough exterior shed.

We sat and talked business, ate dinner, and drank wine. Time had flown by, and I was looser than I realized. I had my legs draped over Cru's lap as we talked about the divorces we both had just gone through. Somewhere along that the conversation we got on the subject of my sex language. I had never been asked that question before, so I had to really think about what exactly it meant and what my answer was.

"My sex language is passionate, adventurous, dominant, and fearless," Cru said, staring me intensely in my eyes.

"Why do you care to know my sex language, Mr. Campbell?" I asked curiously.

"As a man, it is my job to please. In order to please a woman, you need to know her sex language. I never beat around the bush, Ms. Brooks. I'm forward and straight to the point," he replied while running his hand up my thigh.

My words were stuck in my throat. The heat rose with each breath I took. My thoughts were running with ways he could please me. I was burning with lust, and he had my freshly shaved kitty running in anticipation of the pleasure he would give it. I couldn't deny my attraction and what I wanted to happen. I wanted him to take me, bend me over, and deep stroke me until I reached a body rocking orgasm. I hadn't realized that my eyes were closed, and I was biting my lip as these thoughts ran wild.

"Tell me what you want, Kaienne?" Cru said into my ear.

"I don't know," I nervously replied.

"Tell me what you want me to do to you, Kaienne. What can I do for you?"

He began to lower the top of my dress slowly and sensually, taking his time while admiring my body. He looked at me with lust and passion burning in his eyes. I stood still not speaking any words while I let him pull my dress down to my feet where I stepped out of it. He sat back on the couch just gazing over all of my curves. I felt the nervousness setting back in as I thought about how I looked and being on display. I hadn't had a man touch me and want me in so long that I was questioning my ability to be good in the bedroom.

"Answer my question, Kaienne?" he said again standing up and tracing my harden nipples with his finger.

I felt like I was floating on a cloud and my breathing grew harder with each breath I took. Locked in an intense stared I saw myself riding a wave of pleasure provided by Cru and before I knew it my visions had caused me to step out of my comfort zone and throw caution to the wind. I was in heat and needed this more than I had thought. My body was drawn to him and it was as if he was commanding me with no words at all. My body was reacting to him without my control.

"Please me," I said sensually above a whisper, and stepping out of my dress fully I wrapped my arms around his neck before kissing him deeply. It was no turning back.

COMING SOON

L. RENEE'S CATALOG

L. Renee's Catalog

All titles available on Amazon Kindle

Losing Lyric Part 1

Once Upon A Hood Love: A Brooklyn Fairytale

I'll Be Home For Christmas: A Holiday Novella
Enticed By A Real Hitta Part 1

Follow L. Renee on Social Media

FB: La'Nisha Renee

IG: Lrenee418

Goodreads: L Renee
Amazon: L Renee

CPSIA information can be obtained
at www.ICGtesting.com
Printed in the USA
LVHW021454090819
627129LV00001B/164/P

9 781079 382952